SCÉALTA

Other titles in the series

Kahani: Short Stories by Pakistani Women

Afsaneh: Short Stories by Iranian Women

Galpa: Short Stories by Bangladeshi Women

Povídky: Short Stories by Czech Women

Qissat: Short Stories by Palestinian Women

Hikayat: Short Stories by Lebanese Women

SCÉALTA

SHORT STORIES BY IRISH WOMEN

Edited by

Rebecca O'Connor

TELEGRAM

British Library Cataloguing-in-Publication Data
A catalogue record for this book is available from the British Library

ISBN 1-84659-003-5
EAN 9-781846-590030

This edition published 2006 by Telegram Books

TELEGRAM
26 Westbourne Grove
London W2 5RH
www.telegrambooks.com

Contents

Acknowledgements

'Hammer On' and 'Here, Now' were first published in the *Dublin Review*; and 'Men and Women' was first published in *Antarctica* (Faber & Faber, 1999). I would like to thank Shirley Stewart and Brendan Barrington for their invaluable advice and support in putting this collection together. And thank you to Matthew Hollis for helping me to say what I mean.

Introduction

Some people have the gift of the gab. They can transform the mundane into something magical. It's not the local newspaper or the radio we turn to for this kind of entertainment – for the colourful turn of phrase, the unique take on things that changes subtly with each new telling – it's to the storyteller.

The stories collected here make you sit on the edge of your chair, crane to listen. Here are women unabashedly making themselves heard above the din, with sometimes bawdy, always intricately rendered tales of lives and loves; tales as fantastical or as true as you like. This is not a chorus of voices singing harmoniously; it is more akin to a group of session musicians, each taking a turn with the tune, and making it their own.

Most of the people in these stories are ordinary; they do ordinary things – wash the dishes, fall out of love. Where these stories are extraordinary is in the telling, in the minutiae – the cotton weave, the dust motes – of daily living. Ordinariness, of course, is not always good, as in Cherry Smyth's story, in which a child is swept up in a romance with a paedophile, or Eithne McGuinness's 'Feather Bed', where the young protagonist's mother induces her to do unspeakable things.

That there are so many children's voices here is interesting. Childhood is where life takes its darkest turns, at the hands of irresponsible or cruel men and women. It is as if, now at liberty to say what they please, these writers seek to uncover the same suffering that their mothers, and their mother's mothers, experienced behind closed doors. This attention to the domestic scene does not come from a lack of engagement with the grander political or global arena. The broader issues, such as gender and race politics, are literally brought home to us. Of course it's not a new phenomenon, but it is noteworthy here.

As well as children's narratives, there are men's – several of them. Abusive husbands and fathers remain, but men are as vulnerable to these aggressors as women. They are also as susceptible to feelings of loss, alienation and guilt, as with Rashid in 'Pirates', living far from his native Iran to be close to his alienated girlfriend and only child; or Tom, in Julia O'Faolain's story, dealing with his own complicated feelings about his sexuality.

Then there are those characters that seem so far removed from what we know to be 'ordinary' but that somehow bring us closer to an understanding of ourselves – Judy Kravis's solitary figure in 'Dearest Everyone', waiting in the Hotel Furkablick for the snow to rise above his window; or the woman in Anne Haverty's 'Fusion', watching a man, his girlfriend and their dog gradually merge into one. The terrible anxiety of life, its awful absurdity, is exquisitely expressed through their prismatic view.

Among the contributors are one actor, one soprano, teachers, poets, novelists – as various in their experience as the characters in these stories. And the themes they explore – violence, dysfunctional family life, love, grief, exile – are treated with such indefatigable humanity that it's impossible not to be moved.

I could go on. There is so much here to enthuse about. But, rather, I leave you to listen for yourself – to bold new voices alongside those who have been long fine-tuned, and to those that whisper conspiratorially, urging you to come close.

Lean in.

Rebecca O'Connor

Judy Kravis

Dearest Everyone

I'm writing from my old room in the Hotel Furkablick. I'd like to say they still keep it for me, but it would be truer to say that I keep it for them. The eye meets the sky, the sky clings to the ground, and the ground to the snow till there are no more inventions, no fresh people, in fact no people at all. I see to the place as much as I'm able. I like to have a programme of work. I stoke the boiler, open and close the shutters, clear the snow in front of the door, watch the snow fall again and the drifts rise. I scarcely go down to the village any more, let alone the town. I've forgotten, would you believe, the colours of traffic lights, whether the green before the red or vice versa. There are deliveries once a week from the village, except when there's a blizzard, which has been the case for the last two days. This may be the storm that empties the food cupboard, opens the shutters, and lets me out into the real Alps. I tuck my scarf into my jumper. What will the snow wind bring this time? You can smell the chill coming over the ridge, in January as in May. We addicts of the frozen world, we quicken.

As I pause, my room comes forward in its light Furka presence.

Down to this, I say to myself, or up. This long, slow performance, this old age, so much dust displaced for so much longer than I could have imagined. I have been retired for as long as I worked. Add to that the twenty years of growing, getting my schooling, six years of having my war, and there you have me, layered and labelled like a bottle of coloured sand from the Holy Land.

And, Dearest Everyone, there I have you, a warm tribe on the move in whose midst I may one day be carried, some of us puppets, some of us human, some of us dead. Will you come and pluck me from the Hotel Furkablick as you cross Europe? Sometimes I sense you at the window, framed by snow, in your caps, hoods and scarves, all of you, peering in to see if I am there, if I am ready to go.

In the many years I was a father, I did not understand what freight was on it, what fell off along the way, when, or why, or which trucks were cruising on empty. I grew a family, yes, but I don't see their faces at the window. I don't see their photographs, though I took them, though I filed them chronologically on a shelf. I liked the idea of being a father. I sat at the top of the table, I asked for the salt. I look back and that's what I see. Too much salt. I sat there ringed with avoidance, like an ad for toothpaste; after supper I go out to my shed, a scarf tucked into my jumper, and make and mend like a boy with homework. Every day I thought: these children are passing through, they do not meet my eye, they pull in their breath and their attention as I pass by, they wait for nothing as ardently as the day they leave, and then they're gone.

In the vast middle years of family life it appeared that I was not speaking to the rest of the family, or they were not speaking to me, none of us knew why any longer. Impossible to know who had started it. No one would give in. We survived on the belief it would exhaust itself one day. Then after the children have gone there's another kind of silence at the dinner table: you retire and retire again from what you took to be your life.

My wife took a slow and specific leave of life; she forgot food and then the outside world, time and then place. I came to enjoy looking after her, taking her pulse, reminding her to take her pills. I came into my own as she went out of hers. More than half a century it took. Something took. You can be with someone all those years and not know what's taking. Then one day you're putting pills on a saucer at three-hourly intervals and taking her pulse, and then you know.

The Hotel Furkablick has ripened and reduced in concert with my life. I have as many new parts as the hotel, perhaps more. The rooms here have stayed bare and wooden, the plumbing fitful and slow. The wrought-iron balconies are still there, and the faded two-tone paint on the shutters, but it's more a *hütte* than a hotel, by now, a platform to the high peaks. There's a spring-release you don't notice when you first arrive. Slow-release, like certain pills. I like hotels, don't you? As tidy a concept as you could wish. All the solidity you need to be temporary. In this world.

The Furkas understood. They wanted to stand a thousand thousand times on the same mountain; the less they could see of what lay below, the better they liked it. Their hospitality was plain, verging on austere. The guests dwindled, then the maid left, and the cook, Frau Furka died and then there was just Herr Furka and the cats, then the cats, then me.

Herr Furka had a good style in smoking jackets and containment; he wrote a page or two every night and then burnt it in the sitting room fire. Zen and the art of novel writing up in smoke. That made him laugh. If it was a novel. He walked, he chopped wood. He cleaned. He read. Some evenings I saw him listening to Schubert *lieder* in their sitting room, stroking the cat and gazing at the fire. Then one day he went out for his walk and didn't come back. About three years ago now.

I came here for my usual fortnight the year after my wife died, and I won't go back now. The nieces and nephews are in dispute about Herr Furka's will. I'll stay on until the courts below or the courts above settle one or another. I may not have made my peace but I've signed the treaty. You can laugh if you like, but I always wanted to give people the world, every time. To feel that warmth come back. Who doesn't want to be adored? I heard someone say on the radio this morning, and I had to sigh. I have two views on adoration: first you feel as if you can breathe, and then, outside, the world is a chilly place. I speak of my mother now, when I speak of adoration. I could do no wrong in her eyes. A mother is a kind of addiction I suppose, a mess of little strokes, a sine qua non for the puny boy within.

Do you know how I hate saying this? Some of you do. One empty buffet after another. A gale in a cul de sac.

It's easy to see defences when they've fallen, when the darkness has overrun, and the snow is piling halfway up the window, gathering moonlight. I have worn some disguising prose in my day. I will wear some more. Here it is, Dearest Everyone, the current costume, a little *lederhosen* of a letter. *Guten abend*, come in, sit down. Look at the fire. *Sei mir gegrüsst*. Choose a book. Settle in. These days I want my reading to take me home, I make sure of that, into the land beyond the absentees, men without qualities, inside lost time, out on a limb. I've had enough of stories. Can you hear the ice crack, the lichen crumble?

You came round to dinner, Dearest Everyone. You stayed the weekend. We talked, we argued. We drank coffee. I read the Russians then, and Thomas Mann. I unearthed the condition of man, I belonged to CND, went on their marches and helped at their jumble sales. I learned Marxism and Woodcraft and I met you, some of you. We were already massing back then, harbouring decent thoughts and a measure of loneliness. Touching the optimism as we touched the tragedy.

With the years, I moved from a cup of tea after work to a gin and tonic, and my stories began to ripen. Stories were free. They were voluminous. You could work them up. No arguments here. You captured your audience, you won. What a rush I had, holding my own over – please allow me a rather good burgundy. Never a story that I couldn't cap. Allow me that too. We're eating and drinking, and the truth is, I panic. You have told your story and I must tell mine. I sit up straight, I throw my head back, my hands are on the table, my head is trawling the history of the world. I want the moment shiny, the wine warmed and the buzz rising; I want to overcome the sorrow and the seediness, collect everyone up in the choice of my wines, the comfort of my house now opened and filled. I'll bring you with me, but we'll not look each other in the eye. There will be such gulps of admiration I'll be spluttering too, and then, by a miracle, I'll carry on.

Why is this night different from all other nights? This story? Why?

I'm sure you've all seen me seize the air and then, shoulders slightly off-balance and head to one side, retreating almost, anticipating the void I'll hit when you all go home and there are the dishes and glasses to clear up, as well as the fear that you were not entertained after all. Always a huge, a significant story I had to tell, the best, uncappable, triumphant. The silence when you'd gone was cracky and dark.

For Esme With Love and Squalor has lurked at the back of my mind since I first read it here in the Hotel Furkablick. There they are together, love and squalor, the life with the soul at the party, my mother with my father, my wife with my own abject terror. Oh yes, if we're talking of underbellies, we're talking terror, we're fighting squalor from one direction and love from another, a seediness that has lurked about the house, in the kitchen, the bathroom, the practical places, the intimate. There was shame to be overcome from the beginning; there was prosperity to ease into slowly, and then came the era when the sorriest tale was a legitimate fiction.

My mother would have been proud that I could keep an audience of educated people hanging on my words. Listen to him, mine son. She had the art of sighing and shouting, thin swathes of relief language, you know, like the roads that avoid towns but are always full, a kind of Yiddish-with-English-and-Russian rustle of complaint and fury. She had worked hard on my behalf. She would marry me as far upstream as she could, as she had my sister. She would get her son his just desserts, and hers. She waited on her boy, she found me the oysters on a chicken's hips, she watched me eat and willed the puny boy to grow.

My wife in her turn squeezed the oranges and grated the carrots, she chopped the garlic. Healthfulness gathered in the steam. The times I saw my face in my soup, took in my nutrients with my pride, and ached. My mother and then my wife. All those family meals I ate in silence. I have my own silence now, a pleasant downwardness as I seek out the inner morsel the way my mother taught me. And still I prepare my plate, eat the centre, leave a frame of debris, as if weariness overtook me, or distaste.

I'm fidgety, if there were anyone else here I'd probably take a photograph. Always had an itchy clicky finger. I keep getting up and sitting down again. No, let's not squirm out of this one.

I started this letter to all of you, Dearest Everyone, with the intention of coming clean. None of my usual hysterical eloquence, not a joke, hardly a quote from higher sources. No, I'm looking for the name on the closed door, and what do I see? My mother on the road out of Russia, raising her head higher and higher till a princess arrived in London for her day of marriage, which followed on fast. I see my sister, older than me by a couple of years, who went forth beribboned amid her clothes, waiting to be seen and then seized. I do not see my father, yet. I see myself in army uniform, a handsome fella now, my mother thrilled. It was a strange relief, slightly shameful.

I'm enclosing the picture of the hotel taken by that young photographer who came in the early nineties. He captured the isolation, the floating quality of a closed building high in the Alps, without land, without sky. I like the way the roof of the old shed points up towards the hotel, and together they launch into snow lift. Snow is the face of the world here. You learn to read it as you learned to read a mother's face. A suavity, a long saddle of whiteness such as you ride in dreams. You could go deaf, poking your ears into that whiteness. And under the whiteness the strangeness, under the strangeness the centre of the world.

Let us form a void and be happy there.

We used to discuss mountains, Herr Furka and I, the attractions of their shapes, whether it was grandeur or comeliness we admired most, whether they were for scaling or for being there, the mountain and the human, the unutterable distance and then the oneness, which was why you wanted to be that high up and alone. Monte Rosa my favourite. Mountains were such a relief, such a satisfaction that your dreams, your aspirations should stand so solid and graceful. And then you could climb up, uncomprehending, out of breath, the thinness of the air a relief, as ever.

The great advantage of being a stranger in a strange land – apart from the lovely tones of those words – is that you can feel observed and ignored in quick succession. Whatever you say, whoever you are, everything goes out with a change of tablecloth. A hotel is a forgiving place. Our combined savours over the years mingle into anonymity.

Every day I wrap up the cutlery in napkins. Only mine now. There's a pile of them on the sideboard still, gathering dust, that I wrapped the morning of the day Frau Furka met her end in the kitchen. She was standing at the sink, looking out of the window, one hand in the water, the other on the way to a pocket, who knows. I saw her fall forward towards the window, her face registering absolute surprise, snow shock, as if this were a new ending to a book she'd barely begun.

Sometimes I think there is no further clarification to be had, and then more of it eases into my brain and I feel drunk, swirling with revelation that I have found just by sitting here, in Frau Furka's favourite armchair by the kitchen stove. Undifferentiated revelation. She was a kindly woman. I think she saw through me straight away. Where she stood, where she sat, none should enter. She was complete. When you come in from skiing, indoors is like the first room you ever saw. You have the gleam off the snow in your eyes still and then there's a figure moving about the kitchen, into the dining room, or sitting in her chair, in a dimness and a warmth that are irreproachable. She pulled calm into the spot where she was, and you gravitated there.

Is Frau Furka walking with you, or has she gone her own way?

You, Dearest Everyone, who marched against the Bomb, who drank the good burgundy, who stiffened, glazed and wanted to leave, you may not wish to collect me. That is a thought and three-quarters. As you move slowly to and fro between the mountains and the seas, as you cover the great marsh of our Europa, our bull's back, you may know I'm here and go on past.

I would be happy to die in a hotel, a room number on my key and my belongings down to a couple of bags. I would like to think your faces will be there, massing sweetly at the window one day, framed by snow, which, I suddenly notice, is now with an 's'.

There's something I've been trying to do in recent weeks. We've been having heavy snowfalls. Often as not when I open the shutters in the kitchen in the morning I look out onto falling snow. I've read that if you look out onto falling snow you will have the impression that the room is rising rather than the snow falling, in the same way as you can imagine, in a stationary train being overtaken by a moving train, that you are the party moving. I have been trying, waiting for the snowfall to become still and the room to rise, but I do not know if I have achieved it fully. There are moments, and then all is fast flux and anxiety once again.

In your progress across Europe you will not have gathered up my father. Alone, among the silence and the squalor. He had reached his threescore years and ten, or perhaps not, he did not remember the beginning, he had not known the middle and he would not miss the end of his life. There was a sunkenness in his face by then, though that may have been the drugs. He was well medicated in his later years, whether because his polar pulses were more extreme or for some other medical reason I've since forgotten. I haven't forgotten how they argued over the funeral. What did it matter? I've always hated religion.

You know that, don't you, we've all always had that in common?

My father was a salesman, small goods, you know, ties, shoelaces, shirts, belts, braces. He too could be the life and soul of the party. Like the flurries that build the Monte Rosa, my father is a man of snow. He had episodes. And the icy truth, somewhere there under the drawer marked Elastic, is that I must have always thought I'd have episodes too. Instead I had all the subterfuge. When I visited him in hospital, there he'd be, holding thin air in front of the TV screen. He stared through me as he stared through the TV. I was not the reason he was being processed like this. I wasn't any reason at all. He had not journeyed this far to find me, nor would he wave when I left.

Let's take mountains and my mother. Let's take snow shock and my family. Glaciers and my father. Let's take any two things and discuss the difference between them –

The phone just rang. It was the shop in the village to say that deliveries were not going to get through today. Ah well. There's a fair supply of tins still, and I'm working my way through the wine cellar. A glass or two of wine in the evening. I have not found it easy to accept – anything.

As I take the first few sips of wine I feel better. There's some slippage, which will take the place of acceptance. There's the scrutiny that preceded the rock of ages and the first ripple that came after the flood. I am between, rocking in Frau Furka's chair. They were also asking me, the people in the shop, if I'd heard the latest on Herr Furka's will. Apparently he's left the building to the mountain. Some dream he always had, about the rock reclaiming the rock. A shift in tectonic plates, an open maw, sudden warmth and then the Hotel Furkablick swallowed up. This does not gel with the nephews and nieces, we gather. No, it gels with the mountain.

There's a lull in the storm and a last grey light soaks into the snow on the windowsill. I like the moments before dark. Absorption at its height, don't you think? Frau Furka used to say the end of the day was the best of the day, all the aromas had gathered. It will snow again tonight. Already the gap between the hotel and the mountainside is dwindling. By morning the kitchen window could be covered entirely. The snow will be falling and my room will be rising. You'll see.

Claire Keegan

Men and Women

My father takes me places. He has artificial hips so he needs me to open gates. To reach our house you must drive up a long lane through a wood, open two sets of gates and close them behind you so the sheep won't escape to the road. I'm handy. I open the gates, my father free-wheels the Volkswagen through, I close the gates behind him and hop back into the passenger seat. To save petrol, he starts the car on the run, gathering speed on the slope before the road and then we're off to wherever my father is going on that particular day.

Sometimes it's the scrapyard where he's looking for a spare part or, scenting a bargain in some classified ad, we wind up in a mucky field pulling cabbage plants or picking seed potatoes in a dusty shed. At the forge I stare into the water barrel whose surface reflects patches of the milky skies that drift past, sluggish, until the blacksmith plunges the red-hot metal down and scorches away the clouds.

On Saturdays, my father goes to the mart and examines sheep in the pens, feeling their backbones, looking into their mouths.

If he buys just a few sheep, he doesn't bother going home for the trailer but puts them in the back of the car and it is my job to sit between the front seats and keep them there. They shit small pebbles and say baaaah!, the Suffolks' tongues dark as the raw liver we cook on Mondays. I keep them back until we get to whichever house Da stops at for a feed on the way home. Usually it's Bridie Knox's because Bridie kills her own stock, and there's always meat. The handbrake doesn't work so when Da parks in her yard I get out and put the stone behind the wheel.

I am the girl of a thousand uses.

'Be the holy, Missus, what way are ya?'

'Dan!' Bridie says, like she didn't hear the car.

Bridie lives in a smoky little house without a husband but she has sons who drive tractors around the fields. They're small, deeply unattractive men who smell of dung and patch their Wellingtons. Bridie wears red lipstick and face powder but her hands are like a man's hands. I think her head is wrong for her body, the way my dolls look when I swap their heads.

'Have you aer a bit for the child, Missus? She's hungry at home,' Da says, looking at me like I'm one of those African children we give up sugar for during Lent.

'Ah now!,' says Bridie, smiling at his old joke. 'That girl looks fed to me. Sit down there and I'll put the kettle on.'

'To tell you the truth, Missus, I wouldn't fall out with a drop of something. I'm after being in at the mart and the price of sheep is a holy scandal.'

He talks about sheep and cattle and the weather and how this little country of ours is in a woeful state while Bridie sets the table, puts out the Chef sauce and the Colman's mustard and cuts big, thick slices off a flitch of beef or boiled ham. I sit by the window and keep an eye on the sheep who stare, bewildered, from the car. Da eats everything in front of him while I build a tower of biscuits and lick the chocolate off and give the rest to the Jack Russell under the table.

When we get home, I find the fire shovel and collect the sheep droppings from the car and roll barley on the loft.

'Where did you go?' Mammy asks.

I tell her all about our travels while we carry buckets of calf-nuts and beet-pulp across the yard. Da sits in under the shorthorn cow and milks her into a zinc bucket.

My brother sits in the sitting room beside the fire and pretends he's studying. He will do the Inter-cert next year. My brother is going to be somebody so he doesn't open gates or clean up shite or carry buckets. All he does is read and write and draw triangles with special pencils Da buys him for mechanical drawing. He is the brains in the family. He stays there until he is called to dinner.

'Go down and tell Seamus his dinner is on the table,' Da says.

I have to take off my Wellingtons before I go down.

'Come up and get it, you lazy fucker,' I say.

'I'll tell,' he says.

'You won't,' I say, and go back up to the kitchen where I spoon garden peas onto his plate because he won't eat turnip or cabbage like the rest of us.

Evenings, I get my schoolbag and do homework on the kitchen table while Ma watches the television we hire for winter. On Tuesdays she makes a big pot of tea before eight o'clock and sits at the range and glues herself to the program where a man teaches a woman how to drive a car. How to change gears, to let the clutch out and give her the juice. Except for a rough woman up behind the hill who drives a tractor and a Protestant woman in the town, no woman we know drives. During the break, her eyes leave the screen and travel to the top shelf of the dresser where she has hidden the spare key to the Volkswagen in the old cracked teapot. I am not supposed to know this. I sigh and continue tracing the course of the River Shannon through a piece of greaseproof paper.

On Christmas Eve, I put up signs. I cut up a cardboard box and in red marker, I write THIS WAY SANTA with arrows, pointing the way. I am always afraid he will get lost or not bother coming because the gates are too much trouble. I staple them onto the paling at the end of the lane and on the timber gates and one inside the door leading down to the parlour where the tree is. I put a glass of stout and a piece of cake on the hearth and conclude that Santa must be drunk by Christmas morning.

Daddy takes his good hat out of the press and looks at himself in the mirror. It's a fancy hat with a stiff feather stuck down in the brim. He tightens it well down on his head to hide his bald patch.

'And where are you going on Christmas Eve?' Mammy asks.

'Going off to see a man about a pup,' he says, and bangs the door.

I go to bed and have trouble sleeping. I am the only person in my class Santa Claus still visits. I know this because the master asked 'Who does Santa Claus still come to?' and mine was the only hand raised. I'm different, but every year I feel there is a greater chance that he will not come, that I will become like the others.

I wake at dawn and Mammy is already lighting the fire, kneeling on the hearth, ripping up newspaper, smiling. There is a terrible moment when I think maybe Santa didn't come because I said 'come and get it, you lazy fucker,' but he does come. He leaves me the Tiny Tears doll I asked for, wrapped in the same wrapping paper we have and I think how the postal system is like magic, how I can send a letter two days before Christmas, and it reaches the North Pole overnight, even though it takes a week for a letter to reach England. Santa does not come to Seamus anymore. I suspect he knows what Seamus is really doing all those evenings in the sitting room, reading *Hit n Run* magazines and drinking the red lemonade out of the sideboard, not using his brains at all.

Nobody's up except Mammy and me. We are the early birds. We make tea, eat toast and chocolate fingers for breakfast. Then she puts on her best apron and turns on the radio, chops onions and parsley while I grate a plain loaf into crumbs. We stuff the turkey and sweep the kitchen floor. Seamus and Da come down and investigate the parcels under the tree. Seamus gets a dartboard for Christmas. He hangs it on the back door and himself and Da throw darts and chalk up scores while Mammy and me put on our anoraks and feed the pigs and cattle and sheep and let the hens out.

'How come they do nothing?' I am reaching into warm straw, feeling for eggs. The hens lay less in winter.

'They're men,' she says, as if this explains everything.

Because it is Christmas, I say nothing. I come inside and duck when a dart flies past my head.

'Ha! Ha!' Says Seamus.

'Bulls-eye,' says Da.

On New Year's Eve, it snows. Snowflakes land and melt on the window-ledges. It is the end of another year. I eat a bowl of sherry trifle for breakfast and fall asleep watching Lassie on TV. I play with my dolls after dinner, but get fed up filling Tiny Tears with water and squeezing it out through the hole in her backside so I take her head off but her neck is too thick to fit into my other dolls' bodies. I start playing darts with Seamus. He chalks two marks on the lino: one for him and another, closer to the board, for me.

When I get a treble nineteen, Seamus says 'fluke'. According to my brother anything I do right is an accident.

'Eighty-seven,' I say, totting up my score. I'm quick to add even though I'm no good at subtraction.

'Fluke!' he says.

'You don't know what fluke is,' I say. 'Fluke and worms. Look it up in the dictionary.'

'Exactly,' he says.

I am fed up being treated like a child. I wish I was big. I wish I could sit beside the fire and be called up to dinner, lick the nibs of special pencils, sit behind the wheel of a car and have someone open gates that I could drive through.

That night, we get dressed up. Mammy wears a dark red dress, the colour of the shorthorn cow. Her skin is freckled like somebody dipped a toothbrush in paint and splattered her. She asks me to fasten the catch on her string of pearls. I used to stand on the bed doing this but now I'm tall, the tallest girl in my class; the master measured us. Mammy is tall and thin but the skin on her hands is hard. I wonder if someday she will look like Bridie Knox, become part man, part woman.

Da does not do himself up. I have never known him to take a bath or wash his hair, he just changes his hat and shoes. Now he clamps his good hat down on his head and looks at himself in the mirror. The feather is sticking up more than usual. Then he puts his shoes on. They are big black shoes he bought when he sold the Suffolk ram. He has trouble with the laces, as he finds it hard to stoop. Seamus wears a green jumper with elbow patches, black trousers with legs like tubes and cowboy boots to make him taller.

'Don't trip up in your high heels,' I say.

We get into the Volkswagen, me and Seamus in the back and Mammy and Da up front. Even though I washed the car out, I can smell sheep-shite, that terrible smell that always drags us back to where we come from. Da turns on the windscreen wiper, there's only one, and it screeches as it wipes the snow away. Crows rise from the trees, releasing shrill, hungry sounds. Because there are no doors in the back, it is Mammy who gets out to open the gates. I think she is beautiful with her pearls around her throat and her red skirt flaring out when she swings round. I wish my father would get out, that the snow would be falling on him, not on my mother in her good clothes. I've seen other fathers holding their wife's coats, holding doors open, asking if they'd like anything at the shop, bringing home bars of chocolate and ripe pears even when they say no.

Spellman Hall stands in the middle of a car park, an arch of bare, multi-coloured bulbs surrounding a crooked Merry Christmas sign above the door. Inside is big as a warehouse with a slippy wooden floor and benches at the walls. Strange lights make every white garment dazzle. It's amazing. I can see the newsagent's bra through her blouse, fluff like snow on the auctioneer's trousers. The accountant has a black eye and a jumper made of grey and white wool diamonds. Overhead, a globe of shattered mirror shimmers and spins slowly. At the top of the ballroom a Formica table is stacked with bottles of lemonade and orange, custard cream biscuits and cheese and onion Tayto. The butcher's wife stands behind, handing out the straws and taking in the money. Several of the women I know from my trips around the country are there: Bridie with her haw-red lipstick, Sarah Combs who only last week urged my father to have a glass of sherry and gave me stale cake while she took him into the sitting room to show him her new suite of furniture. Miss Emma Jenkins who always makes a fry and drinks coffee instead of tea and never has a sweet thing in the house because of something she calls her gastric juices.

On the stage, men in red blazers and candy-striped bow ties

play drums, guitars, blow horns, and the Nerves Moran is out front, singing *My Lovely Leitrim*. Mammy and I are first out on the floor for the cuckoo waltz, and when the music stops, she dances with Seamus. My father dances with the women from the roads. I wonder how he can dance like that and not open gates. Seamus jives with teenage girls he knows from the vocational school, hand up, arse out and the girls spinning like blazes. Old men in their thirties ask me out.

'Will ya chance a quick-step?' they say. Or 'How's about a half set?'

They tell me I'm light on my feet.

'Christ, you're like a feather.'

In the Paul Jones, the music stops and I get stuck with a farmer who smells like the sour whiskey we make sick lambs drink in springtime, but the young fella who hushes the cattle around the ring in the mart butts in and rescues me.

'Don't mind him,' he says. 'He thinks he's the bee's knees.'

I imagine bees having knees and think it queer. He smells of ropes, new galvanise, Jeyes Fluid or maybe I'm just imagining it. People say I imagine things.

After the half-set I get thirsty and Mammy gives me a fifty pence piece for lemonade and raffle tickets. A slow waltz begins and Da walks across to Sarah Combs who rises from the bench and takes her jacket off. Her shoulders are bare, I can see the tops of her breasts like two duck eggs. Mammy is sitting with her handbag on her lap, watching. There is something sad about Mammy tonight, it is all around like when a cow dies and a lorry comes to take it away. Something I don't fully understand is happening, as if a black cloud has drifted in and could burst and cause havoc. I go over and offer her my lemonade, but she just takes a little, dainty sip and thanks me. I give her half my raffle tickets but she doesn't care. My father has his arms around Sarah Combs, dancing slow like slowness is what he wants. Seamus is leaning against the far wall with his hands in his pockets, smiling down at the blonde who hogs the mirror in the Ladies.

'Cut in on Da.'

'What?' he says.

'Cut in on Da.'

'What would I do that for?' he says.

'And you're supposed to be the one with all the brains,' I say. 'Gobshite.'

I walk across the floor and tap Sarah Combs on the back. I tap a rib. She turns, her wide, patent belt gleaming in the light spilling from the globe above our heads.

'Excuse me,' I say, like I'm going to ask her the time.

'Tee-hee,' she says, looking down at me. Her eyeballs are cracked like the teapot on our dresser.

'I want to dance with Daddy.'

At the word 'Daddy,' her face changes and she loosens her grip of my father. I take over. The man on the stage is blowing his trumpet now. My father holds my hand tight, he hurts me. I can see my mother on the bench, reaching into her bag for a hanky. Then she goes to the Ladies. There's a feeling like hatred all around Da. I get the feeling he's helpless but I don't care. For the first time in my life, I have some power. I can butt in and take over, rescue and be rescued.

There's a general hullabaloo towards midnight. Everybody's out on the floor, knees buckling, handbags swinging. The Nerves Moran counts down the seconds to the new year and then there's kissing and hugging. Strange men squeeze me, kiss me like they're thirsty and I'm water.

My parents do not kiss. In all my life, back as far as I remember, I have never seen them touch. Once I took a friend upstairs to show her the house.

'This is Mammy's room,' I said, 'and this is Daddy's room,' I said.

'Your parents don't sleep in the same room?' she said in a voice of pure amazement.

The band picks up the pace. 'Oh hokey, hokey, pokey!'

'Work off them turkey dinners, shake off them plum puddings!' shouts the Nerves Moran and even the ballroom show-offs give up on their figures of eight and do the twist and jive around and I knock my backside against the mart fella's backside and wind up swinging with a stranger.

Everybody stands for the national anthem. Da is wiping his forehead with a handkerchief and Seamus is panting because he's not used to exercise. The lights come up and nothing is the same. People are red-faced and sweaty, everything's back to normal. The auctioneer takes over the microphone and thanks a whole lot of different people and then they auction off a Charolais calf and a goat and batches of tea and sugar and buns and jam, plum puddings and mince pies. There's shite where the goat stood and I wonder who'll clean it up. Not until the very last does the raffle take place. The auctioneer holds out the cardboard box of stubs to the blonde.

'Dig deep,' he says. 'No peeping. First prize a bottle of whiskey.'

She takes her time, lapping up the attention.

'Come on,' he says, 'good girl, it's not the sweepstakes.'

She hands him the ticket.

'It's a, what colour would ya say that is, Jimmy? It's a, a salmon coloured ticket, number seven hundred and twenty-five. Seven two five. Serial number 3X429H. I'll give ye that again.'

It's not mine, but I'm close. I don't want the whiskey anyhow, it'd be kept for the pet lambs. I'd rather the box of *Afternoon Tea* biscuits that's coming up next. There's a general shuffle, a search in handbags, arse pockets. The auctioneer calls out the numbers again and it looks like he'll have to draw another ticket when Mammy rises from her seat. Head held high, she walks in a straight line across the floor. A space opens in the crowd, people step aside to let her pass. Her new, high-heeled shoes say clippety-clippety on the slippy floor and her red skirt is flaring. I have never seen her do this. Usually, she's too shy, gives me the tickets and I run up and collect the prize.

'Do ya like a drop of the booze, do ya Missus?' the Nerves Moran asks, reading her ticket. 'Sure wouldn't it keep ya warm on a night like tonight? No woman needs a man if she has a drop of *Powers*. Isn't that right? Seven twenty-five, that's the one.'

My mother is standing there in her elegant clothes and it's all wrong. She doesn't belong up there.

'Let's check the serial numbers now,' he says, drawing it out. 'I'm sorry, Missus, wrong serial number. The hubby may keep you warm again tonight. Back to the old reliable.'

My mother turns and walks clippety-clippety back down the slippy floor, with everybody knowing she thought she'd won when she didn't win. And suddenly she is no longer walking, but running, running down in the bright white light, past the cloakroom, towards the door, her hair flailing out like a horse's tail behind her.

Out in the car park, snow has accumulated on the frozen grass, the evergreen shelter beds, but the tarmac is wet and shiny in the headlights of cars leaving. Thick, unwavering moonlight shines steadily down on the earth. Ma, Seamus and me sit in the car, shivering, waiting for Da. We can't turn on the engine to heat the car because Da has the keys. My feet are like stones. A cloud of greasy steam rises from the open hatch of the chip van, a fat brown sausage painted on the chrome. All around us people are leaving, waving, calling out 'Goodnight!' and 'Happy new year!' They're collecting their chips and driving off.

The chip van has closed its hatch and the car park is empty when Da comes out. He gets into the driver's seat, the ignition catches, a splutter, and then we're off, climbing the hill outside the village, winding around the narrow roads towards home.

'That wasn't a bad band,' Da says.

Mammy says nothing.

'I said, there was a bit of life in that band.' Louder this time.

Still Mammy says nothing.

My father begins to sing. He always sings when he's angry, pretends he's in a good humour when he's raging. The lights of the town are behind us now. These roads are dark. We pass houses with lighted candles in the windows, bulbs blinking on Christmas trees, sheets of newspaper held down on the windscreens of parked cars. Da stops singing before the end of the song.

'Did you see aer a nice little thing in the hall, Seamus?'

'Nothing I'd be mad about.'

'That blonde was a nice bit of stuff.'

I think about the mart, all the men at the rails bidding for heifers and ewes. I think about Sarah Combs and how she always smells of grassy perfume when we go to her house.

The chestnut tree's boughs at the end of our lane are caked in snow. Da stops the car and we roll back a bit until he puts his foot on the brake. He is waiting for Mammy to get out and open the gates.

Mammy doesn't move.

'Have you got a pain?' he says to her.

She looks straight ahead.

'Is that door stuck or what?' he says.

'Open it yourself.'

He reaches across her and opens her door but she slams it shut.

'Get out there and open the gate!' he barks at me.

Something tells me I should not move.

'Seamus!' he shouts. 'Seamus!'

There's not a budge out of any of us.

'By Jeeesus!' he says.

I am afraid. Outside, one corner of my THIS WAY SANTA sign has come loose, the soggy cardboard flapping in the wind. Da turns to my mother, his voice filled with venom.

'And you walking up in your finery in front of all the neighbours, thinking you'd won first prize in the raffle.' He laughs and opens his door. 'Running like a tinker out of the hall.'

He gets out and there's rage in his walk, as if he's walking on hot coals. He sings: *Far Away in Australia!* He is reaching up, taking the wire off the gate when a gust of wind blows his hat off. The gates swing open. He stoops to retrieve his hat but the wind nudges it further from his reach. He takes another few steps and stoops again to retrieve it but, again, it is blown just out of his reach. I think of Santa Claus using the same wrapping paper as us, and suddenly I understand. There is only one, obvious explanation.

My father is getting smaller. It feels as though the trees are moving, the chestnut tree whose green hands shelter us in summer, is backing away. Then I realise it's the car. It's us. We are rolling, sliding backwards without a handbrake and I am not out there putting the stone behind the wheel. And that is when Mammy takes the steering. She slides over into my father's seat and puts her foot on the brake. We stop going backwards. She revs up the engine and puts the car in gear, the gearbox grinds – she hasn't the clutch in far enough – but then there's a splutter and we're moving. Mammy is taking us forward, past the Santa sign, past my father who has stopped singing, through the open gates. She is driving us through the fresh snow. I can smell the pines. When I look back, my father is standing there, watching. The snow is falling on him, on his bare head, and all he can do is stand there clutching his hat.

Caitriona O'Reilly

Amour Propre

Self-love. *Amour Propre.* Or, more properly, self-respect. This is something I have never understood. Perhaps it was omitted from my make-up, the wiggly tail of some essential chromosome, forever gone bye-bye. Or perhaps it was leached out of me in childhood, as the Americans would have it. *Got Parents? Then You'll Never Lack a Scapegoat.* It's even better if they abandoned you in childhood, of course, whether because of death or infidelity. Then you'll enjoy a lifetime of pinning your assorted guilt, inferiority, Oedipus, or Electra complexes on someone who can never answer back, like a blindfolded kid at a party trying to pin the tail on a donkey. Daddy, that bastard, he really did fuck you up.

You'll notice I appear to be preoccupied with tails. Perhaps it's because I was born without one. It's not that I envy men their penises; I have always thought that carrying around such a visible sign of sexual arousal, a red flag mechanically hoisted at the first sign of dangerous currents, must be a terrible trial. On dates, back in the days when I used to go on them, I would occasionally find myself staring pointedly at a boy's trousers, just to find out whether he could stand me. It didn't matter a damn what tripe he was talking, the one-eyed trouser-snake never lied. It used to make me feel like a dowser, or like some kind of sibyl. It is no coincidence, I've often thought – though I never wrote an essay on the subject for fear of shocking my Classics professor – that the very first inhabitant of Delphi was a giant snake, later replaced by a woman too crazy to understand the significance of her own observations. And of course sometimes, if a man spots you eyeing his groin, that acts as a catalyst. Which fouls up the experiment in a most annoying way. More often than not, though, they just cross their legs and sit there looking self-conscious. Maybe this is why I never had much success with men. They are fond of directness, but in its proper place, which is in bed. Before and after, they prefer you to be ill-defined, a little blurred about the edges. And I can't blame them for that, since I too would like the world around me to be nice and soft, like wax, the better to receive my impressions. Only it isn't. It's hard and sharp and angular, and its edges impinge.

I remember my mother's puzzlement the first time she heard Whitney Houston's 'The Greatest Love of All', with its unexpected denouement. My mother certainly did not think that learning to love yourself was the greatest love of all. I suspect she thought Whitney might be singing about instructing oneself in the subtle art of masturbation, and she thoroughly disapproved. 'That's rubbish,' she said. 'That just gives people a license to be selfish.' It was the same when we discussed the meaning of the word hedonism, which I'd just looked up in the dictionary. It seemed like an ideal religion to me, and I said so. My mother disagreed. 'But what's wrong with pursuing happiness?' I asked. My mother said there was a world of difference between happiness and pleasure, and that hedonists were after the latter. I professed myself unable to see the distinction. 'Never mind,' said my mother darkly, 'you'll understand better when you're older.' So many things were relegated to this abstract place, this floatel for embryonic ideas, that I always thought my mother should have had a formal, abbreviated response for my more awkward questions, like the English Prime Minister: 'I refer the honourable gentlemen to my previous answer.' It would have saved both of us a lot of time.

The nuns never warned us about self-abuse, probably because in its female form it was simply unimaginable, located on the obscure outer reaches of decadence and therefore partaking of shadowy myth, along with fellatio and the murder of John Paul the First. Although I do remember Sister Mary Magdalene saying once, 'girls, *never* let a man into your mouth.' I puzzled over this for a long time, imagining hordes of tiny men, like intrepid jelly babies, climbing over my chin or abseiling from my forehead in an attempt to get past my pearly whites. I think I concluded that Sister Mary Magdalene had suffered a temporary syntactical aberration, like a glitch in a computer programme, and had really intended to say something else. I had by this time looked up *oral sex* in the dictionary, knowing that if there was a name for something then it had to exist, and I couldn't conceive that Sister Mary Magdalene had ever even heard of such a thing, let alone admitted in public to knowing about it.

No, I am not one of the world's great masturbators, and profess bemusement at the obvious self-enjoyment of others. It's a bit like extreme ironing; some people get a kick out of taking a Moulinex and a pile of crumpled washing to the summit of Mont Blanc; I don't. Such a lot of fuss about nothing. If I touch myself at all, it is with nervous fingers, examining myself for protrusions or excrescences that have no business being there. Once, observing a raised white scar on my arm, the doctor told me I had proud flesh. I thought he was joking until he explained that it was a technical term meaning the over-enthusiastic healing of a wound. Zealous my flesh may be, but it is not proud.

It's easy to be someone like me in this country. The weather here is so terrible that you are never forced to wear T-shirts and shorts, so you can avoid having to shave your legs every week. The shaving of legs, pubic mound and armpits is something I long ago decided I was not going to participate in. The constant effort involved in maintaining oneself in a state of ideal hairlessness has never appealed to me. It's not just that I'm lazy, it's that I have always kicked against it as a complete waste of my time. I'm indifferent to my scrubby bits, and since I am a celibate, I have no one else's instinctive disgust to take into account. I never swim, and so avoid the collective gasp of horror that would accompany my appearance at the shallow end, resembling a pasty, hirsute larva. I never wear short skirts or transparent tights like other women. I couldn't now – should I want to – arrive at a state of mutual nakedness with a man, for fear he should vomit at the sight of my unkempt herbaceous borders. (I've heard it said that some men like hairy women, but I've never met one). And I *never* travel to warm countries. When I was nineteen I spent a summer in Barcelona as an *au pair*, and had a terrible time.

Spain was the opposite of me.

Everyone walked around half-undressed, smooth-limbed, honey-skinned and fuzz-free.

Which is another thing. Why do women's magazines always describe female body-hair as 'fuzz,' as though it were something delicate, almost pleasing, like the down on a bumble bee's back? It is exactly hair, coarse and deeply rooted, especially so around the nipples, as though an ugly daddy-long-legs crouched at the edge of each pink star.

In Spain, I sweated acridly through my blouse and cotton trousers, enduring the repeatedly expressed incomprehension of those around me. In the end, I gave up and came home early, ostensibly because the couple I worked for were both raving alcoholics, in reality because I was obstinately determined not to submit to the razor. I have never ventured south of Wexford since.

I learned a long time ago that I am an invisible sort of person, and likely to become more so. This is because I am not a beautiful woman. I am not even attractive. During my teens, after my features had changed from baby-cuteness and assumed their proper, adult proportions, I noticed that none of the boys showed the least interest in me. I watched the jigsaw of myself gradually resolve into a coherent image, until the indisputable fact of my plainness occurred to me like the first dull ache of a bad tooth. I think I was depressed for about a week, before realising there was nothing to be done. I wouldn't say I forgot about it, exactly. I still notice that men do not stand back ostentatiously to allow me to pass them in doorways, or smile at me in lifts. And this is not self-pity. I despise those obese tantrum-throwers on Oprah Winfrey, whining about how it's not their fault they weigh sixty stone, it's because they felt ugly in their teens, so food became their best friend: 'I knew the refrigerator would never let me down, even if everybody else did.'

Boo hoo.

I am not like that. For one thing, I'm not fat. And for another, I don't lack sexual experience.

I met Victor in the call centre where I worked just after graduating. All of us were filling in time, servicing debts, paying extortionate rent for decaying bedsits in Georgian squares that were gradually being reclaimed for the city's corporate class. Most of us felt panicked, out of step, and tried to remind ourselves, as we fielded the abuse we received nightly over the telephones, that this was just a stop-gap before better things. We watched the friends who had scoffingly told us that the kind of degrees we wanted were a waste of energy buy their first cars and put down payments on their first houses. It was a bad time.

Victor had just finished his H.Dip. and was applying for teaching jobs all over the country. He seemed to like me. In fact, he appeared to find me irresistibly sexy. I went along with this for about six months, enjoying his body more for itself than for what it could make me feel. I liked watching him. He was not especially handsome, but there was something so good and honest about the tension in his body before he came, and his almost childish delight and gratitude afterwards. I was touched. I felt the tiniest bit sorry for him, as though he were a little boy who was going to grow up and find out that there's no such person as Santa Claus. We were both very excited about each other at first, and experimented with all sorts of positions and techniques. It was like starting to learn another language and discovering that you're already fluent. This was when I finally understood the difference between pleasure and happiness. I shaved regularly.

We never lived together. He used to visit me at my bedsit or I would call round to his. We would have spaghetti and a bottle of cheap wine and we would go to bed. Then, after about six months, my body stopped wanting him, and there was absolutely nothing I could do about it.

'Jesus Christ, you're tight as fuck,' he would say.

Eventually, there was no getting inside, and it began to hurt like hell whenever he tried. We did other things instead and that kept him happy for a while but he always returned to the subject, like a child picking at its scabby knee. Eventually he used the word *frigid*, which occasioned our one and only row. After an hour we kissed and made up and I went on my knees before him. He liked that, but Sister Mary Magdalene would have been appalled.

Three days after this our boss rang me and said that Victor had had an accident on his bike. A car had hit him as he was turning into the road outside the call centre, after his night shift, and had knocked him flying. He was in hospital with a broken arm and collarbone, and concussion. His life was not in danger. As I put down the phone my eyes were blurry. I wanted to catch a taxi and speed across the city straight away to visit him, before realising I couldn't possibly do this. His family would be there, and they had never met me. Neither of us had introduced the other to our parents, as if hedging our bets. We had been secret people. So I got up the next morning and ate my nut cluster cereal and went out to work as usual. To people who asked me how Victor was I said, *sedated*. All that week the feeling grew on me that I had in some way been responsible for the accident. I wondered what Victor had been thinking about as he turned into the road and into the path of that car. I suspected it might have been the word *frigid*. My intention had been to visit him after a few days but as the week progressed I felt heavier and heavier, as though the material of my body was being converted into some dangerous metal. I told myself he would blame me and not want to talk to me. I told myself I would be upset by the sight of him lying there with a bruised face and the arm of his pyjamas slit up to the armpit to make way for the plaster of Paris. By Friday I was convinced he would be better off without me and that same day I gave a week's notice at the call centre. Nobody paid much attention; their staff-turnover was high. I went on the dole for a while until I got another job in another call centre. I sent Victor a letter telling him I'd seen him in the hospital while he was unconscious and that it had made me think I wasn't any good for him. I wished him a speedy recovery. On my birthday, which was two months later, he sent me a card. On the front of the card it said, 'I asked my psychiatrist what I should get you for your birthday, and he said...' and when you opened it, it said, 'an appointment!!' All he'd written was, *from Victor*.

I freely admit it, I suffer from what might be described as a failure of feeling. All my life, at significant moments, I have done the wrong thing, emotionally. Like when I was fifteen and my grandmother was diagnosed with inoperable cancer. I had always been very fond of my grandmother but after I heard what was wrong with her I started to behave as though she was already dead. When I looked at her, propped up on her pillows, her soup spoon wavering because she was almost too weak to hold it up to her mouth, I felt like asking her why she was even bothering to eat, why didn't she lie down then and there and get it over with. She asked my mother what was the matter with me, why was I being cold, when the truth was that I was looking past her, past the six months that the doctors had given her. I saw her reduced to an abstract figure, like those chalk outlines the police draw on the ground around a corpse. She was just someone who would disappear from the face of the earth in six months time. It was as if she had never been my grandmother. We were an unfailingly polite family, however. My grandmother never mentioned the fact that she was dying and no one else mentioned it to her. And, after eleven months – her heart was unexpectedly strong – she did die. Strangely enough, I've never been able to drink soup in public since without getting a dreadful case of the shakes. I usually order a solid starter.

A psychiatrist would undoubtedly put a fancy term, like *depersonalisation*, on this behaviour of mine.

I call it facing facts.

When I looked past my grandmother, past the doctors' conservative estimate of her suddenly reduced life expectancy, I saw clearly what was behind her, and it was nothing. Not nothing as I had known it before, like an expected letter that failed to arrive, or a feeling of boredom, or the absence of noise on the top of a mountain. This nothing was like an enormous grey insect that sucked all of my grandmother's past out of her and left the rest lying there like the dry skin of an orange. It didn't matter that she'd loved her mother or been married at nineteen and had six babies.

It didn't matter that I was her granddaughter.

I didn't matter.

Come to think of it, the death of my *amour propre* can be traced to that moment. It was like a religious conversion. I looked out at the world through different eyes. It was as if a little grime had been cleaned from the windscreen, but the view outside was terrible. It made things like sex and depilation seem completely pointless.

So I watch other women who buy lingerie and have facials and drench themselves in expensive scent, or men who have back, sack and crack waxes, and think compulsively of the phrase 'fiddling while Rome burns.' I confess my lack of *amour propre* even makes me feel a little superior sometimes, if that isn't too much of a contradiction.

Eithne McGuinness

Feather Bed

I thought they'd put me in a little room on my own and when they didn't I was glad. Sister Róisin liked me; said I was a great girl for not making a fuss. I didn't talk to myself, or snore, or wake up screaming in the night. At home, making a fuss led to a beating. To being told to get the wooden spoon and to pull down my knickers.

'This instant, if you please.'

My bare bottom felt huge in our little kitchen. The weight of my dress pressed onto my back and shoulders. My socks bit the soft skin behind my knees. Knickers floppy and disgraceful around my ankles. The blue wooden chair that Daddy painted to match the cupboard was cold and smooth against my belly. The relief when she finally hit me; sharp red pain. We both wanted to get it over quickly before someone – Daddy – walked in. It was our secret. When Daddy was around we pretended to be pure.

I never cried, I'd pull up my pants and climb the stairs. Then I'd twist myself in two in front of the bedroom mirror to count the moon-shaped stains the wooden spoon had left behind. She was always sorry later; she'd stroke my head and tell me she loved me. I didn't believe her. Even if she did, it didn't change anything; the whizzing in my head or the thumping under my vest.

'I love you more than anything in the world, why do you have to be so bold? Is there something wrong with you? Something you want to tell your mammy?'

I didn't know what was wrong with me. I just liked fighting with her and making her wild. It was better than sitting there looking at her painting her mouth red. Better than being left alone in the afternoons when she went 'out'. Better than watching her slide into Mr Naidoo's green Mercedes and having to stay beside the phone when the sun was shining, to tell my father she was gone to the shops if he rang. Much better than the dirty, sweaty smell of her when she came back all shiny.

'Who got you a little present for being so good? Daddy doesn't like you having too much chocolate, so this is just between you and me.'

I stopped eating the chocolate, saved up eight Crunchies, four Lion bars and twenty Curly Wurlys but she wouldn't stop going out. I was eleven years old.

In the hospital, I listened to things and watched people from behind *The Readers Digest.* I read the joke pages and increased my word power. After a week Sister Róisin said maybe I should go home; I didn't seem crazy at all. Next time she tucked me in, I explained all about the baby. She went very quiet. Then she kissed my hair.

'The family,' she said, 'is a breeding ground for character and moral strength. Maybe we'll hang on to you for another week or so, all the same.'

The days were very long. We were only allowed watch telly in the evening but the radio played on and on. Mary in the next bed went mental if anyone talked while Gay Byrne was rabbitting. I told her my mother said he was a louser because he talked down to people, but Mary started to cry so miserably, I let her be. She had a spark in her eyes listening to him; like he lit her up from the inside. Larry Gogan had no effect on her at all, though. She ignored me shouting out the answers to the 'Just a Minute Quiz' – even when I got them right. Larry sounded fair. He was disappointed if people got things wrong, not secretly laughing at them. Larry was the King of Pop; he chose the Top Thirty. I loved the songs he played, especially the ones with lots of verses, that told a story, like *Bohemian Rhapsody* and *Ground Control to Major Tom.*

Angela had the window bed because she'd been there the longest. She was welcome to it. I got a headache trying to see the outside through those bars and the worst of it was, if I was near the window at all, I couldn't stop looking. Seemed like there were magnets in those bars. Angela used to be a hairdresser, said she'd give me a whole new look, if only they'd lend us a scissors. One afternoon, I let her backcomb my hair and Meat Loaf came on the radio. Before I knew it, I was up on the bed, growling into the wide part of my hairbrush with Angela wrapped round my knees. She did the woman's part, 'And will you love me forever?' Even Mary, who was so old she whistled her words, joined in. Banged out the beat with her wedding ring on the white metal frame of her bed.

Dr O'Doherty stuck his neck around the door.

'Down,' he said, as if I was a dog. I just sang louder. He stepped into the room. Angela half-slid, half-rolled off my knees and snuck back into her corner. I kept going, though it was hard work without my backing singers: in fact, I think I went out of tune. O'Doherty looked angry; he came close, right up to my face. I kind of spat at him, I didn't mean to, it was the song – you know the exciting bit about praying for the end of time. He told me to shut up in this low, filthy tone. Then I really did get upset – you don't expect that outside of your own home.

You can tell a lot from a person's eyes, if you're looking. Dr O'Doherty's were glittery and boastful. They made me want to scratch them. I reached out and the shine went right off them. He swung for me. Quick as a flash, I jumped clear; his fist scooped the air. O'Doherty didn't like me because I had my own psychiatrist, paid for by the V.H.I.

'Her own con-sul-tant no less, nothing too good for her ladyship.'

He went to grab me again so I kneed him in the balls. He folded like a wet paper bag. Mary laughed, a weak windy sound. Angela was scared; she started to pray, her mouth wobbling like the brown and orange fish in the dayroom tank. I hated that tank; stupid fish gawping at nothing, darting round and round in murky circles.

O'Doherty was still crouched over. Everything was completely still. I heard Larry introduce the next number – *Julia*, by the Beatles. Julia is my mother's name. I got into bed, pulled the clothes up to my chin. O'Doherty raised his head; his eyes were all watery, just like a baby getting ready to cry. That made me so sad I pulled the covers right over my head.

He made the nurses do my dailies after that, prescribed an extra pill for me to take after breakfast. The first day I stored it under my tongue, Angela laughed when I showed her. I stuck it into a hole in the skirting board. The next day the nurse stood over me, I pretended to swallow. She poked around my mouth, rubbing the chalky lozenge against my tongue as she pulled it out. She rinsed her fingers in my water glass and handed me another tablet.

'Down the red lane like a good girl.'

Angela didn't even look ashamed.

'What did you do that for?'

'If you keep up your messing, you'll get us all into trouble.'

O'Doherty was extra nice to Angela from then on; brought her in some American magazines he said his wife had finished with, and a large bar of fruit and nut. If I spoke to him, he presented me with the crisp white square of his back. I missed him all the same, his *Aqua Velva* smell and the soft fingers on my elbow as he wrapped the blood pressure sleeve around my arm. The nurses' hands were leathery from being in water. The extra pill made me sleepy but it didn't stop me getting up.

My favourite person was Marcella, the cook. She was fat and smelled of brown bread. I didn't eat much but she didn't mind. I explained that my brain only had the power to administer to a certain square inch ratio. If my body got any bigger, my brain would overload trying to control the extra area and I would lose my power.

'Power to what?'

'Exist.' I told her.

She nodded, 'You know best.'

You can see why I liked her; she was a very unusual person to find in a mental hospital, though it was more of a halfway house. It was called Cluain Mhuire, which meant something like the refuge of Mary. There was even a little church, but they didn't let anyone from our ward go to mass in case we caused a disturbance. The optimum calorie intake to keep my vitals ticking over, without any unwanted expansion, was six hundred and fifty. I ate the porridge in the morning – no sugar, just milk. At lunchtime, I usually managed some grey looking meat and gravy, then a boiled egg with triangles of toast for tea.

I had learnt the 'calorific value' of every food from my mother. She went to Unislim on Wednesdays and brought back lists of food with pastel-coloured headings. Yellow and green were good, pink was so-so and red, well you can imagine. On Tuesday evenings, I sat on her feet while she did her sit-ups. She looked like a worm who'd been poked in the middle – both ends wriggling. We walked backwards on our bottoms across the carpet and did scissors with our legs, but mostly she made me count. She said I was good at that. No matter how much she dieted, my mother could not reduce her bust. She held her wrists and jerked the skin back, making them jump with the fright. She said they were a curse, she was a slave to them and they'd be the undoing of her, if she let them.

Marcella's bust was huge; massive batch loaves under her apron. I asked her if she hated them. She said the Lord made her that way, well upholstered, her husband was mad about them, said it was like resting on a cloud.

'How many people can say that?'

'None.' I said.

I leaned up against them, just to see. She felt more like a feather bed to me. Still, I didn't want big ones; Marcella was probably a slave to her husband's desires. He'd always be at her, saying, 'Give us another go on your cloud.' I wasn't going to be a slave to anything.

I saw my psychiatrist on Wednesdays. His name was Dr David Walker. He was so polite and well-spoken I thought he might be a Protestant, but he never let on. Told me nothing. I asked him all sorts of questions during the inkblot and the word association tests, but he was a hard man to draw out. I made him laugh though, he said I was a tonic and that I'd be better off on stage than ... long pause ... 'A loony bin,' says I. That made him laugh more. He asked me what I thought about life and how I thought others saw me. I told him I didn't think people were looking at me at all, that I didn't want anyone looking at me and from now on I'd be keeping an eye out. I had to make things up to fill the hour. I told him I'd been shoplifting in town and that a dirty oul fella in a banjaxed hat followed me down a lane. He smiled and wagged his head at me, knowing well I'd been locked up since the previous Wednesday.

'An overactive imagination,' he said, 'that's all that's wrong with you.'

It was three weeks before Daddy came to visit. I recognised the shape of his head through the wavy glass in the hall door. I ran up and started rapping, 'Daddy, Daddy it's me.'

'Hello love, hello.' He sounded scared. Sister Róisin unlocked the door. Daddy looked like he'd had a slow puncture. In the dayroom he took my hand and rubbed it so absent-mindedly you'd think it was his own.

'Nice place.'

'Not so bad.'

'I wanted to come earlier, but they said it was better to let you settle.'

'Oh.'

'I missed you though.'

'The doctor says I'm a tonic.'

'And your mother, she misses you a lot.'

He stood up and went over to the tank. It seemed easier for him to talk to the fish.

'Says to tell you she can't wait to get you home, wanted to come herself, but she's still not well ... poor girl. Delicate, always was.'

He was such an eejit, hadn't a notion. If he'd seen her bump herself down the stairs, he'd see how delicate she was.

It wouldn't come out. She'd spent hours in the bath drinking mugs of gin and castor oil, sending me up and down for boiling water. Then she told me to put my Wellington boots on. She'd left them in the hall for the tinker lady, who called once a month for things for the babby. I hadn't worn those boots since I was eight. My foot only went halfway in. She sat on the sitting room floor. I just stood there looking.

'Do I have to tell you again? Do I?'

I started to cry. She pinched the soft skin under my arm between her fingers.

'Do it, or I swear you'll be sorry.'

I closed my eyes and kicked out hard, the wellie flew off, hit the mantelpiece, then landed on her head.

'You needn't think I can't see through you. You'd like me to be ruined. Keep your precious Daddy all to yourself. Kick me. Do you hear? Kick me.'

He wasn't there the night it dropped out; it wasn't his hand she squeezed till the knuckles were white as bone. Her head thrown back on the cistern, blue veins pounding around her eyes. The glare off the bare bulb in the outside toilet bouncing off the wiry grey hairs standing to attention on her head. I'd never noticed them before. It wasn't him who had to flush.

'I'm done for, give me a knock when it's gone,' she said, pushing home the bolt on the kitchen door.

It wouldn't go down. I poked it with the handle of the toilet brush. Each time I touched it, sour tea sprayed into my mouth, right up my nose. I thought I saw the shape of a hand, or maybe it was a foot. What if it was still alive? Squirming away from the pointy tip of the brush. It started leaking; tadpoles of blood stuck to the sides of the bowl. It took a long time and half a bottle of Harpic. Mammy opened the door as soon as I lifted my foot onto the step, I didn't even have to knock.

'It wasn't black,' I told her.

'Too early to tell.'

She went to bed. It was Daddy who found me crying and crying in the garden with the drain cover on my lap. I'd fished out dead leaves and slime with a bamboo pole. He picked me up and carried me inside. My mother called the doctor.

* * *

'Are you ready to come home?' my father asked.

'It's not bad here, I might stay another week.'

'Your mammy wants you.'

I went to pack my case.

JULIA O'FAOLAIN

Pop Goes the Weasel

Tom, flat on his back, was using pain to quell his memory.

His arms ached. Above him teetered a weight which he must not let slip. In his mind it was now a boulder. Of basalt. Or limestone. Not that it mattered. What did was the muscle-pain. Grittily, he savoured that. You had, he believed, to conquer yourself so as later, if need be, to tackle the world. His pupils accepted this. Most of them. Only Rafael, missing the point, had once asked if Tom was thinking of the *next* world.

Raffo could get things a tad wrong, indeed he was in jail now for enforcing Tom's principles with excessive zest. He had wreaked mayhem on a pair of badasses. Fellow students said Tom shouldn't blame himself if Raffo lacked flexibility.

'He takes the American dream too much to heart!' they decided.

'Listen, he takes *karate* too much to heart.'

'And the movies!'

'It's being an immigrant.' Gary was the class intellectual. 'If you psych yourself up to adapt to a whole new culture, you'll keep looking for challenges. Raffo wanted to be like those knights in the blow-ups on our dojo walls, Tom. Dragon-slayers! They must have impressed him as a kid. They'd have been some of the first things here he saw.'

Rafael had been in Tom's karate class since his family brought him to L.A. from Mexico at the age of ten. He'd been the first Hispanic to join and the only one to stay.

Tom, while he had nothing against Hispanics, had a test question for them. 'Ever heard of a bunch of Mexicans,' he'd ask, 'who lay claim to California, Texas and everything in between? They call it Atalanta or something like that. Do you know about them?'

No one said they did, but Tom went on putting his question. He wanted any mad Mexicans on whom he might stumble to know their cover was blown.

He didn't get to put it though to Rafael's Mom. She was a Spanish-speaker, brown as gingerbread who, one day twenty years ago, simply appeared at Tom's door with little Rafael, his baby sisters and a basketful of cakes in the colours of the Mexican flag. Raspberry, cream and pistachio! Pure cholesterol! Tinted sugar sifted from the basket; alien smells polluted the dojo and Tom couldn't have said which of his powerful personal taboos was the most acutely violated. A baby started to cry. Soothing it, the gingerbread Mom opened her blouse, thrust her cakes at Tom, and pointed to little Rafael. 'This one,' she said, 'want study karate. Give me no peace. All day watch your class. From there.' Popping one tit into the baby's mouth, she pointed to an apartment balcony overlooking the dojo, then said something to the boy in Spanish, perhaps that he should show what he could do.

Tom expected shyness, but there was none.

'*Kiai!*' yelled Raffo, while performing a creditable middle-level sword-hand block in back stance. A natural! Then he did the splits. An uncle had promised to pay for his lessons.

Later, Tom wrapped up the unwholesome cakes and drove with them to a distant litter bin. He didn't want anyone's feelings hurt, but neither did he relish the smells which lingered in his dojo until he got at them with Listerine. Next day Raffo joined the class and, some years later, got his black belt. Since then, several more years had passed, and pupils from Tom's first junior karate class had now had their black belts so long that the fine Japanese silk had worn thin, and the belts were turning white. About ten old pupils still trained though, turning up three times a week – it had once been six – and Rafael had been one of the most faithful until last month when an unathletic-looking judge sentenced him harshly on the grounds that having a karate black belt was the equivalent of being armed. The guy reminded Tom of his own uncles from Salt Lake City. Stiff! Dry! Convinced of their rectitude. Years ago, two of them had come out here to L.A. for three days, looked down their lean Wasp noses at California, then turned and gone home. Tom got the impression that he, like the state, had been considered and found wanting. On that occasion, however, no judgement was pronounced.

'Remember, Tom,' Gary reminisced, 'how awful Rafael's accent used to be? Martin kept making fun of it until Rafael punched him in the mouth. He broke two teeth and Martin's Mom threatened to sue you.'

'I told her to go right ahead.'

'Yeah!' The class enjoyed the memory.

'Martin's Mom was quite something!'

'So was Martin!'

'Remember how we were all set to testify that he was a mean S.O.B. who had it coming?'

'Martin was worse than an S.O.B. He was a small sadist. What you never saw, Tom, was what he got up to when you turned your back. Especially during sparring.'

'His Mom wouldn't let him train with us after that.'

'But when he was sixteen he came back.'

'That's right! She couldn't stop him then and he'd grown into an acceptable guy!'

'Fairly acceptable.'

'Rafael had taught him a lesson!'

Wham! Nostalgically, Tom dreamed of evils which could be simply knocked out. Flattened! Merdilized! Up-p again! Wondering if he'd heard a bone crack, he steadied the weight. His arms buckled. Effortfully, he raised them once more. As a professional chiropractor and martial artist, he knew how much to demand of his body.

'Push *beyond* your threshold,' was his motto.

In his fantasy the weight was a boulder which could slip, set off an earth slide and block the entrance to a cave from which fugitives had started to emerge. A girl had got out, but something had happened to the man behind her. His face was muzzled in blood, and one of his eyes, veined like a rare orchid, hung as if from a stem.

'Aa-*uuu*-wwawwagh!' Tom's anguished bellow surprised himself.

Embarrassed, he assigned it to a predator deep in the cave. Dragon? Cyclops? No, a giant earthworm. Tom had watched a video once in which a lovely, white-skinned gal changed every night into one of those. The story was by the same guy who wrote *Dracula*. Tom tried to remember his name. Gram, was it? Or Bram? Bram Something? Bellowing again, he congratulated himself on having had his dojo soundproofed. At one time he'd had forty students, and when they yelled '*kiai*' the building shook. Neighbours complained that it sounded like the start of the big L.A. quake. So Tom called the sound-proofers.

Deep in the cave, something phosphorescent glowed. Tusks? Slime? Were the fugitives all safely out? 'Ni-inety-nine!' Tom let sink then raised his barbell one last time. 'A hundred!' Replacing it, he gave a high sign to a movie poster on the wall which showed a man hefting a rock. The man's muscles jutted. A girl, wearing the stone-age equivalent of a bikini, was creeping fearfully from a cave, and you could tell that the man would now lower the rock, corral the evil inside and join her in the sunshine. Tom's fantasies usually stopped there.

Today he held onto them, letting his mind flit through a medley in which the stone-age gal turned up in the *Star Trek* episode he'd watched last night. Slivers of reality knifed coldly in, making him shiver even as he stepped under the hot shower. Again he saw the dangling eye.

It was Jim's.

Tom, embracing numbness, turned off the shower and thought-stream, extracted a karate *gi* from a cottony pile smelling mildly of himself, put it on, took a quart of plain yoghurt from his office fridge and sat down to eat. The stiff sleeves creaked and he felt bolstered by routine. No point ringing the hospital yet. They'd said not to. Jim was in intensive care. Tom who hadn't cried since he was a kid felt a hardness in his throat.

The yoghurt had the clotty texture of a nose-bleed, but he ate it anyway for, as health-lore changed, so did his diet. Gone were the days of steaks and pie. Like his Mormon forebears, he looked to the long run, but, giving up on heaven, subscribed instead to news letters on smart drugs and nutrients and, to keep his brain active, took challenging courses in maths and the biology of ageing in which he already had a PhD. His aim was to stay healthy until researchers into our DNA cracked the code which tells us to die and reversed the message. He believed this to be imminent.

'I'd hate,' he told students, 'to be the last man to go!'

Slyly timed, such remarks let him catch his breath between strenuous routines. Did the guys know, he wondered, and if so, did this embarrass them? In the old days, he would have crucified anyone who said a word during training. His own Japanese *sensei* had run *his* dojo like a boot camp, and for years Tom, honouring the tradition, stayed inscrutably buttoned-up and dignified. Lately, though, he had been regarding his students as family and sharing his thoughts.

The changes went back to Heppy's death. Mom's. Mrs Fuller's. Her ghostly selves gusted back if he didn't take measures – and must at some point be dealt with.

Crumpling his emptied yoghurt carton, he let one bad memory oust another. This morning, out on the boulevard, there had been a five-car pile-up. Sun-blurred after-images floated in and out of focus, hiding then brutally highlighting bone shards puncturing a cheek, Jim's fierce, extruded eye, crushed metal and a bunch of stunned faces, two of which he knew. A car had been totalled right outside this office while another, somersaulting past the central divider, burst into flames. Tom, hearing the collision, had rushed out and there was the totalled car wrapped around a lamppost and next to it Jim's old jalopy with Jim folded into the steering wheel. In the periphery of Tom's vision, making a getaway in his BMW, was an intact but tight-lipped Martin.

Martin! Tom got the picture instantly: those assholes had meant to fake it! Holy shit! They'd planned to fake injuries and walk off with the insurance money. Martin must have talked Jim into it. Tom could imagine his spiel: 'Listen! Listen! Your old lady's busting your balls. Your car's worth zip. Just say you have a whiplash neck. We'll get Honest Tom the Chiropractor to back you up. He'll believe you and the insurers will believe *him*. We'll do it right by his office. The symptoms are a cinch to fake.'

Jim, a mild, handsome ex-lifeguard with a knee injury, was

one of Nature's fall guys. Before the knee injury he had married a gal who kept nagging him to get off his butt and do something. But Jim didn't see what he could do and had been in here joking miserably about this. She'd made him use their savings as a deposit on a house, and he couldn't keep up the payments. He'd flunked law school and lost a job as security guard because of his limp.

Tom, hating to know about scams, averted his eyes from so much that, for a while, his disbelief in ambulance-chasers, snuff movies and markets-in-stolen-hearts-and-kidneys had equalled that with which other people greeted his hopes of living forever. The difference was that when *they* had evidence, he bowed to it, which was more than they did to his. This amazed him. Awesomely, human immortality had begun to look attainable and, bafflingly, his students didn't seem to care. Tom harangued them with wonder. Just last week, Martin's pale little eyes had blinked impassively while Tom talked right through the limbering-up period.

Why, he marvelled, were they not ecstatic! Their generation could – Tom delicately stretched his hamstrings – be thirty-plus forever. Didn't they grasp the privilege? Didn't they – here he happily, though still delicately, swung a kick in the air – want immortality? Making imaginary contact, his bare toes trembled at high noon.

'Listen, I'm in my sixties, and *I* want it!'

In the training mirror, his levitating self reminded him of a prophet ranting in some souk! Prophet or monk. His crew cut had acquired a tonsure. Or some white, arrowy, Japanese bird.

'Hey,' someone – Martin? – guffawed in the back row, 'if nobody dies, the planet'll get overcrowded. They'll have to ban sex!'

'Yeah! *You'll* have to be castrated!' Aiming humorous assaults at each other's groins.

'It should be done now. Aids is the warning!'

'Aids! Yeah! Yah!'

'Don't touch me man! Keep your body liquids to yourself!'

'Sex-maniacs should be interned!'

'Or at least banned from the dojo!'

Feinting and dodging, kicks snapped, punches were pulled and white sleeves furrowed the air like paper darts. Rowdiness was how Tom's class stopped him wasting paid-up time in talk. Only rarely, in retaliation, did he assign them five minutes' squat kicking – high kicks from a low squat, like dancing Cossacks – then, when he had them winded, returned to his topic.

Doing this had once drawn a taunt from a flagging Gary – less fit than he liked to pretend: 'Tom! Know why immortality appeals so much to you? It's because you don't live life! You save it up.'

The verbal punch to the gut took the others' breath away. How could it fail to in a dojo devoted to the values of Southern Cal? The hush, compounding unease, lasted until Gary, in a manoeuvre learned from Tom who trained actors to perform it in movies, floored a phantom assailant, then whirled to demolish other lurkers – among them, surely, an unworthy self?

Tom was flummoxed. In what way did he not live? How? What could Gary mean? The attack was the more hurtful because Tom liked to be joshed. Lately, aiming to Americanise karate, he had tried to behave less like a sensei and more like a genial uncle who attended students' graduation parties and welcomed them back after their divorces – matrimony tended to interrupt training.

As a chiropractor, treating the unfit among them, he no longer nagged when their flesh proved softer than his own. Jim was one of these, a slack, needy man whom Tom should have protected. He should have warned him against Martin who last June had made some startling admissions right here in the dojo.

It was just before class. The day was hot and the door to the boulevard had been left open to cool the place down. Suddenly a collision – like a small try-out for this morning's – happened so close that the men catching the breeze had a ringside seat.

'Hey! Look!' Gary had been a rubberneck since he was ten.

'*Diosito*!' Rafael reverted to Spanish.

'Faked!' decided Martin after a quick glance. 'Half of all accidents are.' Then he told how teams of bogus victims, paramedics, lawyers and doctors – 'or', with a foxy grin at Tom, 'chiropractors' – divvied up insurance money.

Later, privately, he offered to cut Tom in, as he was apparently in a position to do. There was a lot, 'And I mean a *lot*,' said Martin, to be made. 'If you don't grab it, others will.'

Tom was less shaken by the dishonesty which he knew to be rampant than by Martin's failure to see how genuinely *he*, Tom, cared about honour. Karate, he always scrupulously taught, was as spiritual as it was physical. It was why he had chosen, decades ago, to perfect himself in an art which, at the time, few Americans understood. 'Kara' – 'empty' – referred not only to the fighting man's hand but to his need to empty his inner self of ego, leaving it as straight, clean and hollow as a green bamboo shoot. Clearly, despite years of training, this message had not reached Martin. Was the fault Tom's?

Had he, softening, let his own egotism back in? Undeniably, he had mellowed and was sometimes startled to recall a self who had favoured interning peaceniks and keeping fags and women in their place. These aims baffled him now – which did not mean that he thought right the same as wrong.

'Stop right now!' In a panic of refusal, he tried to shut Martin up, 'Stop! You mustn't say things like that around the dojo!'

'OK then! Have it your way!' Shrugging, Martin opened the door of Tom's office in which this talk had been taking place.

'Well,' he exclaimed, 'Just look who's outside!' Amused. He tilted his chin towards the car park where Gary was clearly on the watch. 'Your protector's worried, Tom! Afraid I'll stir you up and get you really mad. Give you a stroke maybe? I'm still the badass in this Castle of Virtue!'

Tom *was* mad. Stung, he warned, 'I ought to turn you in. How do you know I won't? Ten years ago I would have.'

'Ten years ago I wouldn't have told you.'

Tom turned that over in his mind. Martin had intuition: a thing you had to respect. Seeing idealism die, he had adapted and that, like it or not, was evolution. It was how humanity survived. He'd surely survive better than Gary who couldn't see beyond the tip of his own argument. Words, to Gary, were only words and films films. He and Tom battled over this and last Monday, when Tom was probing the significance of the videos he had watched over the weekend – *Batman*, which he'd seen for the tenth time, and *Bladerunner* – Gary had cut in with a 'Tom, those are films! That's all they are!'

Tom couldn't let this pass. Mindful of the jibe about his not living, he had argued with more assurance than he felt, 'No, no! Films tell you what the trends are. That's why you got to watch them. With all the brains and money that go into them, they have to reflect current thinking. Violence is going to take over. That's their message. Breakdown. It'll be every man for himself. I don't worry. I have my guns. I've always been a rugged individualist. I'll stop being a chiropractor if they bring in socialised medicine. I wouldn't work for that. I'd get another job. Adaptation is the name of the game. Individualism. Being self-sufficient.'

For Gary this was the sort of daydreaming which had brought down Rafael.

Was it?

Wrapping an old T-shirt round a broom, Tom buffed the dojo

floor while casting an occasional glance up at the dragon-and-knight images on its walls. He hadn't really looked at them in years and, now that he did, was surprised to find the dragons – robotic, feral, breathing fire – more impressive than the knights. Martin, with his fiery accidents, was a sort of dragon. Or a Merlin: a faker who even faked himself. Tom guessed that he took steroids, for his muscles were oddly swollen. Poor Rafael, though he had shown the valour of a knight errant by single-handedly giving three nasty guys their come-uppance, did not look at all like the knights in Tom's blow-ups.

These bestrode their space. Their muscles thrust past armourplating whose scaly bristle made them too look dragon-like. The effect was futuristic and medieval: a blend Tom enjoyed. It was as though the future held the best of the past in store: Paradise Two, a sequel to Eden. Later would come the Fall.

'It's coming,' he kept telling his class. 'There were several films about it recently.' He mentioned the actresses' names. 'Great-looking gals!' As his listeners savoured this, he pulsed with their breathing pattern. Gals interested him most at a remove. 'There's a trend.'

'Tom, those are *films*!'

'No! Films,' Tom had insisted, 'are real!' He corrected that. 'They anticipate reality. The thinking that goes into them does.'

Putting away his broom, he wondered who would come to class today. Not Martin, not Jim, not Rafael. Then the door was pushed open and there was Gary with a gal whom Tom recognised as Rafael's wife, Elena. Small but feisty, at one time she'd started training here, then decided she'd be better off in a women's self-defence class. Tom, not really wanting women around, had been relieved. He liked her though, and she had been very good about visiting his mother in her last months. The two, surprisingly, had grown close and Elena had spent whole days with the dying woman.

Greeting her, he asked about Rafael and was told he was bearing up.

It turned out she needed a favour. With Rafael in jail, the bank had foreclosed their mortgage and taken their house, so now they had nowhere to store their furniture. It was in a truck outside. Could she leave it here?

'Just for a bit,' she begged and explained that she hoped to rent a place soon.

'It could go upstairs,' Gary told Tom, 'in your mother's old apartment.'

Six months earlier, Heppy, Tom's mother, had died, leaving a clutter of Norman Rockwell plates, flimsy side-tables with sugar-stick legs and knick-knacks so alien to Tom that, after shipping what she'd asked him to ship to cousins in Salt Lake City, he had given the rest to the Salvation Army. Only the room where she had spent her last months was intact. She'd had a house in Pasadena until her arthritis got bad and Tom brought her here where he could keep an eye on her during the day. She had died upstairs. Maybe it was as well to crowd out her ghost.

'Sure,' he agreed.

So instead of a karate class, there was a furniture-moving session with everyone who turned up for training pitching in. Tom relished the sociability, as neighbours dropped by, containers too big to move were broken into and objects piled on his strip of lawn. As in a garage sale, private things were incongruously displayed. A chest-expander lay between a picture of the Virgen de Guadalupe, a juicer and a bathroom scales. A long package was possibly a rifle, and a box of cakes was an offering from the girl whose misfortunes had sparked off Rafael's troubles. Elena introduced her: Juana. They were cousins. Tom, though he hadn't met her until now, knew her story from Rafael and the *L.A. Times*.

He tried not to stare. She couldn't be more than sixteen.

'Just fourteen when it happened,' Rafael had told the class. Gangsters, he explained, had kidnapped her from her village in Mexico, then smuggled her here to L.A. to be a sex slave.

'Slave?'

'Slave! She was a *slave*! They paid her nothing and kept her locked up.'

'You're having us on!'

'No.'

'What sort of gangsters?'

'Small-time ones. They own a bar in East L.A. where they made her work.'

The scenario seemed to belong to another place and time. Tom imagined the young Liz Taylor as Juana whose age suggested a fanciful romp with periwigs and tricorn hats. 'Yer money or yer life, yer ducats or yer wife!' Or an ad. 'Pray, take these instead,' cries the captive girl, offering brand-name chocolates to the heavies who lower their muskets, lick their lips and accept the bargain. In a darker mood, your thoughts could slide to the stolen children whose hearts and kidneys are allegedly sold to rich or desperate First World parents.

The reality was less harrowing since, by the time Rafael heard of it, Juana had been found. Her family, into which he had meanwhile married, had known who to blame – *pistoleros* who had moved to Los Angeles – so her brother, though himself a child, had set out in pursuit. Making his way across the border then, though he had neither money nor English, to the L.A. *barrio* where people from his part of Mexico lived, the boy had succeeded in picking up the trail of the men who, with violent thrift, were using and abusing his sister as maid-of-all-work and whore.

'So he got her home? Back to Mexico?'

'Yeah, but it took a while.'

'What a feat though! Like Samson and Goliath!'

'The newspapers helped. They made a story of it.'

'How old did you say he was?'

'About like the kid in *The Thief of Baghdad*?'

'Or *Les Miserables*.'

Without movie-world lore, the thing would have been too alien to understand. As it was, the class had to look with a new eye at their old pal, Raffo, who must, they now saw, have a Mexican border slicing through his mind: a division as hard to negotiate as a Rio Grande in flood.

'*Pan Mexicano*?'

Juana was offering cake. Oozing cream from a sugary slit, it looked even less salubrious than the ones with which Rafael's mom had failed to tempt Tom twenty years before. Juana had removed her jacket and revealed blue-veined arms. A waif. A Dickens girl. Her skin, he saw from close up, was poor. Probably ate the wrong diet and needed further salvation. In a film, the make-up people would have provided this, and Tom, to his amused surprise, imagined himself transfiguring her, as the orphaned Little Lord Fontleroy had been transfigured, in a lace-collared velvet suit. Instead, he accepted her cake and a coffee – Elena must have unpacked her own percolator, for he never drank the stuff – then walked off to find somewhere to rid himself of both.

* * *

The kidnappers, Raffo had told the shocked dojo, had gone scot-free. They must have done a deal with the police, though naturally he didn't know details. Maybe they were stool pigeons? Part of an undercover anti-drug or smuggling squad? Juana was sure some of the clients she'd been forced to service were cops. By now the newspapers had lost interest – or been warned off?

Vigorously kicking the air and, with it, the dreamed-up faces of *pistoleros*, the class considered their society's loss of virtue. When had the rot set in? Kick. With President Kennedy's death? The cover-up? Kick. Water- or Irangate? Kosovo? Kick, kick and kick again! Somewhere faith had been lost. Mislaid. Roundhouse kick.

'Again with the other leg,' encouraged Tom. 'Add a backfist to the face, elbow strike, upper block and back kick. Pulverise the opposition. Yell *kiai*! Turn. Keep together! More spirit! And again!'

Few of us, he reflected, were the straight bamboo shoots empty of selfishness that we would have wished. The scourges and avengers. The new brooms. Excited advice, though, was lavished on Rafael – most of it, Tom saw with hindsight, unwise.

He tried to recall what he'd said himself, but was interrupted by Elena who wanted to be shown how to use the barbecue. Next came a debate over who should go to the store for refreshments and what they should buy. Beer? Mineral water? Juice? Tom didn't join in.

There was a debt owing to that girl. 'A debt outstanding!' Hearing the words hammer in his head, he wondered if they were his words to Raffo? They had a boom, which reminded Tom of his father more than fifty years ago. A pillar of pinstriped darkness looming up to make him cry. Acrid-smelling. Fuming and unpredictable. 'Young man,' it scolded, 'you owe ... owe ...' What? To whom? 'To me,' boomed Pop, and slid menacingly into focus. 'And you'll pay, young man! I'll see to that. Don't cringe! Cringing doesn't impress me. I have a duty to bring you up right, even if your mother spoils you. A duty to society!' Stiff collar. Stiff-judging mouth. Huge, terrifying fist. Slamming down, it blocked out the light as Tom fell on his back and his ears rang from the blow. Strong smells of alcohol. Once Pop dislocated

Tom's shoulder. Then, somehow, he died and Tom and Mom came West. In the train, she sang a rhyme, which Tom misinterpreted:

> A penny for a cotton ball,
> Tuppence for a needle!
> That's the way the money goes,
> And POP goes the weasel!

Bang! Blow Pop away! Pop-the-Weasel! Wasn't that what had happened?

Maybe the voice in Tom's head was an echo of his own? 'This city's lost its virtue.' That was his all right! He must have been remembering the lost, radiant, Pop-free L.A. in which he grew up: clear air, innocent leafiness, sun spraying like yellow petals and nothing to be afraid of. Even in the canyons the only danger was from coyotes, which would eat a baby, if its mother was an airhead and wandered off, leaving it on a rug. There had been one such case, he recalled – but things went wrong in Eden too. Eden. The jacaranda trees seemed to unravel the sky when their blossoms opened in a blaze as blue as the sea – which was there too, rippling like shaken silk. Warm and salty. Luminous, unpolluted and safe.

'We're safe,' his mother whispered, 'safe, safe, safe and we'll never go back. Never! We'll stay here together.'

So they did. She wasn't the sort of mother who'd leave him alone on a rug. Nor he her.

* * *

Elena, back from the store with charcoal and lighters, paused to watch Gary fix the barbecue and to tell Tom how much more culture meant to Mexicans than it did to people here. 'That's why Rafael is so impressed by your studies. He used to tell me how when you talked of the things you cared about, it went right over the heads of the class. It went over his head too but he loved listening. And he admires your beliefs. He says you are one of the last men to have principles the way the great Americans did. Ah, good, Gary's got the fire going. I'd better bring the food.'

* * *

Dusk found Tom sitting at the head of a table – Elena's table which had been set up in his mother's dining room – picking at takeaway Mexican food. From politeness, he let *fajitas* and *chilli relleno* be piled on his plate, and a bottle of Mexican beer placed next to it. *Dos X*s. The two women were to spend some nights here. Gary had brokered the decision while Tom was ringing the hospital where Jim turned out to be less badly injured than had been feared. He was in a stable condition and could have visitors soon. Tom asked about his eye but the gal at the other end of the phone was slow-witted and didn't seem to understand.

He was pleased to see Juana eat. She was not at all like the small Elizabeth Taylor, but thinnish and frail like a plant in need of a stake. Her wrists were the size of his two middle fingers and there were shadows under her eyes.

Watching him watch, Elena whispered, 'She had to leave home and come back here because of the disgrace. People were calling her the gringos' whore.' Her brothers, murmured Elena, were treated as pimps, even the one who'd rescued her. 'She needs someone older to look after her. Don't you like those *fajitas*? There's no fat on them.'

Tom said sure he did and put some chicken on his fork. Cancer, he remembered reading. They buy the good bits of cancerous chickens and cover them with chile. He hid the chicken under some onion. No way would he eat this.

'You don't eat much,' said Elena, catching him.

Tom said he'd had something earlier.

'Juana starved herself when she got home,' said Elena. 'Trying to get rid of her ass and tits from shame at being a woman. That's what the doctor said, so her mother sent her to me. It's not a convenient time to have her, but how could I say 'no'? She can't go back there. There's nothing there anyway.'

'I suppose not.' Tom thought of a drive he had taken to Baja California where the First World meets the Third and green land yields to parched brown. A mile or so south of this, he'd taken a wrong turn into an encampment of derelicts sitting by a bonfire. It was dusk and the air was thick with ashes or maybe bats. Some of the derelicts stood up and closed in on his car. They waved their arms menacingly – but were bought off with the price of a few beers.

Pocketing it, they'd looked shrunken and forlorn and the thought grazed him that maybe they'd merely been directing him to the nearest hotel, a place where you could drink margaritas and listen to mariachis while the sun set over the Pacific. Where else would the gringo driver of a car like his be heading? He had no Spanish, and money, his only currency, seemed to disappoint them. Perhaps they had been hoping for news of the First World which, though inaccessible to themselves, was just up the road?

'Rafael,' Elena was saying, 'sees you as his model. His father is jealous. He never liked his doing karate.'

'Why not?'

Elena looked uncomfortable.

'Does his father blame me for Rafael's trouble?'

'Sure he does, but don't let that bother you. It's how Chicano families are! The parents are fearful but the kids want to stand up for themselves. Rafael thinks of you as his North American father. Really! And your mother was a heroine for me too. Heppy! So brave when she had to defend you from *your* father. She told me how he'd get drunk and beat you senseless until she was sure he'd turn you into an idiot or maybe kill you, if she didn't kill him. And how then she had to explain this to a jury which had been turned against her by photographs of his head with the eye hanging out like a loose knob. I'm sorry, am I upsetting you? No. I know you're proud of her. She had such courage. And heart! *Corage y corazon*! She was such a small woman, no bigger than Juana, yet she told me she snatched up that statuette without thinking whether it would do the job – or of what would happen if it didn't. It was just there on a side table and could have been made of anything – ceramic, glass, but she was lucky and it was made of lead. That helped with the jury. That it wasn't premeditated. Oh, I'm sure even they admired her. Anyway they found her innocent. That was great – even if she did have to leave home later. Like Juana. Juries try to be fair but gossip doesn't. Do you know that if I'm letting Juana stay with me at a time like this, it's in memory of Heppy?'

While she talked, Elena was removing plates and bringing on a 'flan'. Some sort of custard. Taken up by her reminiscences, she said no more about Tom not touching his food. He felt badly about that, recognising a primitive violation of – what? Solidarity? Also he was hungry. Maybe that stuff about cancerous chickens wasn't true? Too late now to change his mind. Elena had scraped the plates into a garbage bag. Pinkish refried beans mingled with tomato sauce. The business about his father's eye shocked him. Had he suppressed it? Tried to give it to Jim? 'Hanging out like a loose knob?' Yes, that was how it had been. A drooping tassel. On whom? Jim? Pop? For moments their heads fused and swam inside his own. Nacreous and messy, the eye swayed unattributably. What colour had his father's been anyway? Pop's popped eye! Now back in its socket, it lit up in Tom's memory and scanned him knowingly. It expressed pure rage and Tom was dazed with fear. Behind Pop's head, Tom's mother raised the statuette and he, despite his daze, saw – and stayed silent until his father's exploding head splashed substances which, later, had to be washed from Tom's hair. Could he have imagined this? Could he?

Blinking, he rose. 'I've got to phone about Jim,' he told the table and went down to his office.

'How about his eyes?' he insisted when he got through. 'Are they injured?'

He was told that the patient's vision did not seem impaired. Tests would be run later but as of now no injuries to the ocular region appeared to have been sustained.

Tom went into the bathroom where he rolled his own guilty eyes at the mirror and threw water on his face. His mother had clearly needed to reminisce and rid herself of her memories, and he'd never let her. Couldn't bear to be left with them himself. Oh well, too late now! Pop goes the weasel! Try and forget it all. They were both dead.

Or should he see a shrink?

He went back up to find Gary leaving along with a neighbour who had helped with the moving and stayed to eat. Elena was loading the dishwasher. She asked about Jim then remarked that he and Martin had been trying to raise money to help pay for Rafael's appeal.

'For that and Jim's downpayment. Well, they blew it. Poor Jim.' She turned on the machine.

Its heave echoed the sensation in Tom's head.

'Are you sure?' he harried on a rising note.

'Of what?'

'That Jim and Martin ...'

'What?'

'Never mind. Excuse me. Must talk to Gary.' He could hear him down below saying goodbye to the neighbour. A car door slammed. Tom tumbled downstairs and out to where Gary's face, gleaming in his car window, vanished, then gleamed again in the blink of a revolving sign.

'Did Jim and Martin plan to raise money for Rafael?' Tom asked.

'Tom, you don't want to know. Ok?' Gary patted Tom's hand, removed it from his windowpane and drove off.

Tom stumped indoors. Back in his own quarters on the ground floor, he looked glumly at his video collection. There was no way he'd get to sleep now. Why did they keep things from him? What was their opinion of him anyway? Reading the video titles like mantras, he tried to calm down. *Four Feathers*, *Oliver Twist*, *Superman II*, *Silence of the Lambs* ... Violence *was* coming all right. *Great Expectations*. Funny how much, even as a boy, he'd liked nineteeth-century English stories. That century had been a manly time for the English. Their prime. Elena had been trying to work on him. She wanted him to see her as in some way Mom's heir.

Really hungry now – he'd eaten nothing since the yoghurt – he opened his office fridge which was empty except for a can of tuna. He was starting to wolf it when there was a knock on his door. It was Elena to ask about locking up. She saw the tuna.

'Oh Tom, you're hungry. You hated those *fajitas*! I could ...'

'Hungry? No, no. I was just tidying. Throwing this out.'

He threw it in the garbage. Rafael's family was always making him do this.

'I'll take that out, then lock the doors. You go to sleep. We've disturbed you enough.'

'No, no, please, don't bother.'

'It's no bother,' she picked up the bag.

Arguing, he followed her through the dojo. He had half a

notion that he might discreetly recover that tuna since the office garbage bag would have nothing worse in it than paper. But she evaded him playfully and seemed to be in high spirits. He remembered that she had drunk several beers.

Pausing to wave at the dragon-and-knight pictures, she said, 'Know what Rafael says, Tom? He says you're "in thrall" – that's his word – "to the dragon of memory". That it's like in some old story about someone who's asleep and guarded by a dragon.' She nodded at a lively monster with a scarlet trim to its jaws and scales sprouting green as grass. 'This made no sense to me, so one time I asked your mom what she made of it – and she began to cry.'

Elena shook her head a few times, shrugged, then smiled, it seemed to Tom, a little sourly and added, 'of course Rafael wants to rescue you.'

Tom didn't understand any of this and had a feeling that he didn't want to either, so he gave up on the tuna and, after saying goodnight to Elena, returned to his room.

Later, hearing her go upstairs, he put on a video, then fell asleep in front of it. Woken by hunger, he decided to go to an all-night store, only to find, on trying the outer doors, that she had taken away the keys.

* * *

Upstairs the rhythm of sleeping breath had changed the place; the temperature was warm and the air musky. Padding about in stockinged feet, he told himself that Elena must surely have left the keys somewhere obvious. Having switched on a light in the kitchen and found no keys there, he followed its slanting gleam into the dining room which smelled of Mexican cloth – that cheesy memory of sheep – a whiff which he remembered sometimes getting from Rafael.

There was a *rebozo* on the table but no keys. Groping, his fingers alighted on flesh and someone gave a tiny scream. It was Juana who turned out to have left the bed she had been sharing with Elena, then fallen asleep in here. In explanation, she showed him the photo-romance she had been reading before turning out the light. Pointing and grimacing, she laughed at her own lack of English.

'Elena took my keys.'

'I sorry. No understand.' A breathy gabble of Spanish.

The whispers were too loud. Tom, who wanted her to look for his keys in Elena's room, led her downstairs in the hope of explaining his predicament by showing her the locked front door.

A prompt, submissive smile told him she'd got the wrong idea. Of course! The photo-romance still in her hand showed a picture of an evil seducer.

'Not that!' Waving agitated hands, he tried to shoo away her misapprehension. Poor girl. She saw men as predators.

She quailed, clearly thinking him angry, so he tried to look well disposed but not predatory. 'It's all right, Juana. Don't worry. It's just that I need my keys. To get out. See.' Carefully avoiding eye contact, he made a show of trying and failing to open the front door. But now her misapprehension changed. Panic clouded her. Was he putting her out? No, no. He smiled reassurance – but this too was open to misunderstanding.

'Keys?' He mimed the act of sliding one into a lock. '*Llaves*? Get it? No?' Frustrated, he flung himself onto the sofa in front of the video where Scrooge – he must have put him on earlier – was embracing Tiny Tim.

'Ah!' she cried, '*que rico*!' And, joining him, cuddled close and took his hand in hers.

He snatched it away then, as she quailed, became remorseful

and led her back up to where a startled Elena awoke, rubbed her eyes and shot him an unwarrantedly knowing look.

'Elena,' he tried to keep exasperation out of his voice, 'Juana keeps getting the wrong end of the stick. Will you please tell her that I'm not putting her out, but that I don't want to sleep with her either?' The voice sounded querulous. He tried to soften it. 'Listen,' he soothed. Yes, that was better. 'Listen, you can both stay here as long as you choose. OK?'

'Oh Tom, do you mean it?'

'I ... oh well, I guess so.'

He went back down to find his TV screen curdling furiously. Turning it off, he realised that they might want to stay for months. Years even. Could he back out? He couldn't. He had, moreover, forgotten to ask for the keys. Could he go up and ask for them? No, he could not do that either. The girls would be in bed again by now. He'd embarrass them – and Juana might again get the wrong end of the stick. Yet he was hungrier than ever and his windows, since he'd had the place soundproofed, didn't open. Sitting on his couch, he could only laugh to think of Rafael in prison, Jim in hospital and himself locked in his own house and dreaming of food. Gary might say he'd always kept himself locked in and on a diet. Well, maybe so.

Upstairs was now silent, so he tiptoed back up, opened the fridge and took out Juana's last remaining cakes which were by now a little crumbly and reminded him of boyhood greeds. Bright and smeary like First Grade crayons and dripping with lipids.

Thoughtfully, he chewed, then swallowed one, two, and finally four with the help of a can of Mexican beer which was in the fridge too, then went down to his bed where he dreamed recklessly that Juana was lying beside him, only to find her turning into Rafael who had the same black, brilliant eyes but was in better shape and had the grace of a healthy feline. The crumbs on Tom's lips were sweet and he imagined a prison-hungry Rafael asking if he might lick them, and himself saying 'Sure.' Rafael saying, '*Hombre*, I'm glad you've started to like *pan mexicano*.' Then, somehow Tom had him in his arms. Why not, he thought, and, feeling himself start to wake up, pulled the dream back over him like a slipping comforter. Why not? Why not stay under here with the smell of vanilla and strawberry and Rafael's smooth, hard body and fresh, athlete's sweat? Because before we know it, *hombre*, pop goes the weasel. The DNA boys aren't moving fast enough, so we'd better be our own Merlin the Magicians – if and while we can. Tomorrow, he though, *mañana*, I'll visit Jim. Then dozed again, with an eager, dreamy hunger, in Rafael's arms.

Later, in a deeper, more unruly dream, he thought he heard himself say one day in class, 'Somebody should teach those guys! Blow them away. Wham!'

Had he? Had he said that? To Rafael? Egged him on? Played Lucifer? He had. He had.

Anne Haverty

Fusion

'Wouldn't you like it?' I pleaded.

He looked at me warily ...

My fiancé has learned to do wary, he does it well and he does it often. I don't mind, I don't mind at all. I don't mind any particular way he might look at me as long as he continues to look. It's not being looked at I would mind.

'Wouldn't you?' I knew I shouldn't insist but I couldn't help it.

'Wouldn't I like what?' Now he was pretending that he didn't know what I was talking about. But of course he knew, my fiancé always knows what I mean. That's why he looked at me 'warily', as I say.

'To be fused.' I said it out, patiently, pretending myself now that I didn't know he knew.

'I fucking wouldn't,' he said. 'In fact, to be honest what I'd like is to be de-fused.'

He would have seen my alarm. Wary possibly?

'I mean de-con-fused,' he said quickly.

'Me too,' I assured him. 'I'd really like to be de-con-fused.'

He clasped his face heavy in his hands and shut his eyes from me. And he sighed in that heavy way that I really don't like at all. He seems so separate when he does that.

'Why don't you go and watch some television', I told him. He likes watching television. Anyway it was coming up to seven and I was chafing to get to my couch. 'You're thinking too much.'

He gave his tired smile. 'Oh? It's me who's thinking too much, is it?'

He stood up. 'Promise me you won't be watching now,' he pleaded.

'I promise,' I said. He would have known it was a bad promise. He knows I have no choice but to watch. But he was nice and went off with himself anyway.

When I could hear the companionable drone of voices from the television in the other room I knew it was safe to take up my place on my little couch. Don't think of me reclining as in 'lolling' or 'curled-up' or slack-postured in any way. On my couch I sit up straight and completely alert. From time to time, to persuade my fiancé that I was engaged in normal housewife-like activities, I would make clunky-clattery noises with forks and knives across the plates and bounce cups and saucers up and down on the dining table, which I had repositioned to be conveniently near at hand. But that was only to be on the safe side. I could be confident that he would be shortly dropping off and I could watch in peace. He always dozes off when he lolls in front of the TV.

You see, I don't want to miss a thing and that could easily happen if I actually did engage in domestic tasks. The kitchen window is totally useless. I've tried. It's tiny so the view is rubbish, and there's nowhere suitable to sit in there, if you're going to be sitting for long. Just the two hard kitchen chairs, and believe me, a person can't afford to be bothered by aches or discomforts when they're watching. You get distracted and then you could miss something.

Not that I was expecting the young man just now. But maybe I would find somebody or something else that could give me fresh food for thought ... I try to keep an open mind. I don't want to obsess, I really don't, I'm at one with my fiancé on that. As I am pretty much on everything. Ninety nine per cent, anyway. But once a thing is set off in your mind ... How can you stop that?

My young man walked the dog between four and five of course, not between seven and eight. But that is only speaking generally. There had been many occasions in the past when a later walk was taken. But that was before, in the autumn and wintertime, when his girlfriend still walked independently by his side, one or other of them gripping the dog's lead as he pranced eagerly along in front. It could vary in those early days when they were still two, in the matters of the timing of the walk, and which of them would take the lead. There was a disorder then, a sense of all that continuous negotiating that people have to endure when they are still two.

Maybe she liked to walk in the dim glow of the streets under the yellow lamps. Or maybe sometimes she worked late and the usual walk would be postponed. I'm sure she worked in a library. Definitely she was the studious type. An intelligent-looking person. Well, now she wouldn't be going to work in the library anymore. She might be glad to be relieved of the job, maybe that was a factor in ...

Not like me. I liked my jobs, of course I did. But what could I do? The mishaps of too alert a perception set me back. I must say my employment as catering assistant on the train suited me more than anything.

Always bang on time – a train is not a thing you can afford to be late for – arranging the refreshments neatly in their places on the snacks trolley, the sandwiches above, nuts, crisps and sundry salteds below, biscuits, bars, sundry sweets below them, the conical tube of cups to hand ... Pushing my trolley forth and back, always bang on time, Dublin to Galway, distributing refreshments to the grateful passengers. They were always hungry, always eager to see me coming. That's what started the whole slide. The slide into ...

Not my fault. They changed my train you see, they re-rostered my route, put me on the Dublin-Cork, and they shouldn't have, they really shouldn't. That was a big mistake, they just should not have done that. Should not have put me on an unfamiliar route. Only the first time going down – going down, that's what alarmed me – I should have been left, you see, on the same line, the straight line of latitude Dublin to Galway. And just outside of the town called Charleville it was clearly apparent to me that we had passed the same meandering river only a few minutes before. My passengers had all been catered for and I was watching, you see. I tried to remain calm despite the beat of my heart drumming and drumming ... It can happen on a plane, I told myself. Okay, that's normal, on a plane you can go round and round and see the same road and the same river ... But on a train? That should not happen on a train.

I tried my best. But when it happened again, when the meandering river loomed into view, exactly the same river only it was winking now in a sinister manner because, you see, it knew I knew, I pulled the communication cord. What else could I do? There was no way I was going to get myself trapped in a vicious circle. With the passengers all ignoring me, acting as if I didn't exist, now they'd been catered for. And the fellow with the laptop who never looked at me at all and robotically devoured his sandwich from one hand, so that he couldn't have enjoyed it properly, as he tapped away with the other ... He wasn't a bit grateful, only came close up to me with a big red glaring face on him and shouted 'I'll see you sacked. You've caused me to miss an urgent meeting'.

'All rivers are meandering', they alleged when they called me up to HQ. As if that was some kind of excuse.

I liked Extresses too, nearly as much actually as I had liked catering the Dublin-Galway line. I was really very contented in the hair salon, pushing the shorn tresses back and forth along the floor, so intensely alive still, so vivacious, companionable ... I did like it until that afternoon ...

It could get so intense in the salon, all the driers going and the taps steaming and the exudations from all the ... I could get intense now even thinking about it. And suddenly it was all illuminated and it came to me how I was walking around on an upstairs floor that all the basins and the people were sitting on, suspended in the air above my terra firma and all so heavy and hot and perilous ... It could go, any minute ... I saw all the rubble and the smashed basins around me and all my limbs gone dead and chalk and dust clogging up all the new hairdos and pools of viscous red clotting in the dust. Or worse, the one above us could go, seeking as was only natural unto terra firma ... Extresses departed who knows where, like a train you've missed vanishing into the western light ... And left all alone in the darkness to face ...

Carefully, so as not to disturb, I took off my duck-egg-blue overall that I had been quite happy in before and walked out of there, never to go back.

'Couldn't you work on a ground floor?' my fiancé asked. 'You could get something in Super Valu. They're always looking for people in Super Valu.'

But it would be the same thing in Super Valu, I had to tell him patiently. Or anywhere else. Once you see the truth, there's no way you can be talked out of it. And you shouldn't let anyone try, not if you're like me and you place any value on yourself and staying part of ... Of course you might be thinking I'm weird, one of those weirdoes, well, you see them everywhere, you can't go out without … But I'm not, not really. I'm not alone you know. There's lots of us, behind the brick, behind our windows, looking, watching, happy at last.

I had been getting quite impatient over dinner. Well, nothing to do now thankfully but get down to my watch. A fix, my fiancé calls it. In the beginning he was cheerful enough. 'You got your fix, did you?'

Later it became 'your fucking fix'. Now watching has no descriptive title. Not to be named, referred to at all, not to be discussed …

Although it was more than unlikely, I warned myself, that he'd show up. The girl preferred a night-walk obviously but she'd have little say in the matter now. Any wish of hers could be easily ignored. It was his long reach after all that took down the dog lead, his large feet that walked behind the dog's stubby paws. But that was the wonderful thing after all. Her wishes wiped, subsumed … That day, I was unusually hassled. He hadn't made his customary appearance between four and five. And to further cause unease, I hadn't seen him the day before either.

All this deprivation was making me think too much. It could be that the girl was gaining the upper hand in the relationship. Not a good idea. Maybe she had won just for today the murmuring internal argument. No, maybe he just wanted to please her? When you thought about the possibilities, there was certainly the chance that he could be along any minute. To be safe I tinkled a knife and fork on the plates but maintained my gaze alert on the panorama of the street. I wanted to check out the hair once more, the lie of the shoulders. The imagination can be deceiving, can't it. I wanted to be sure.

Funny, you know, but also I wanted to be wrong. I was so attracted to the prospect of fusion, oh, so attracted … but there was a part of me that wanted to be wrong. Wanted to be able to go in to my fiancé and shake him awake, and yes, I am sure I could do it even joyfully. To be able to say to him the words. 'I was wrong, I was mistaken.' To have him look at me not warily anymore, but to look in a nicer way. Like the young man looked at the girl.

And I wasn't being unrealistic now because it was in fact between seven and eight that I watched them first. It was soon after I had taken to my place on the couch, when I had given up watching TV, so boring as it is. Boring, boring, boring. No imagination. And they had come along, this young man and the girl and their dog, who was pulling them up every so often to sniff or inspect some scent or other ... And right there by my railings, as I sat on this very couch, the dog pulled them up, having got a whiff of next door's cat, I'd say, and they came to a stop under next door's early cherry – that I consider to be mine actually since the blossoms belong to me, piling up as they do in rotting drifts inside my railings when they fall ...

The way that pair stood there, I found it ... compelling. Yes, compelling is the word. Knowing instantly that what I wanted was to be nestled warmly between ... Chatting away, each smiling into the other's bespectacled eyes. They both had narrow transparent frames to their rectangular glasses. His and hers. So I should say that his wearing now what could very well be her glasses is a proof of nothing. They could just as easily be his glasses.

The two of them stayed there so long in my sights, and illuminated, I would say – yes, illuminated – in the light coming from the new blossoms above, they were lost so deep in each other, I was able to take them in from head to toe. Her hair, shiny and dark but overgrown made me think of Extresses, I remember, and set up in me a complex of emotions, some good, some bad, as they go after such an experience. He was tall, his hair tan-coloured and inclined to be frizzy. We didn't do males in Extresses so I was no way affected on his account. Her eyes dark, round like chocolate drops, his lightsome like a cool sparkly drink I never tasted but could imagine ...

What else is there to say? Regarded separately as units they were like anybody else. 'Common as they come', as mother would say. It was their combination that made them stand out, like two ordinary little scraps of wire that spark up when they're brought together. Their dog was a striking fellow. A large and bulky animal, its coat grey with white spots regularly spaced out along the length of his back. As if it had been designed with a lot of planning beforehand. The dog took them away from me, yanking them onwards on a sudden whim, and the murmur of their talk, like the babbling of a stream in the country somewhere, fell away as they moved out of view.

For a good while I was able to watch them every day, at the one time or the other. As I would see the fat blonde girl with the twin buggy going up and down from the shops at noon. And the business-type man with his briefcase going past at five forty or five forty-five, five minutes give or take on either side. And the Asian lad in his bow tie heading down to his night job in the Blue Orchid. I know all about him because my fiancé insisted on eating out in the Blue Orchid a few times and I was able to pin him down there which was definitely a compensation for having to leave my couch. Lots more, many I've forgotten. I had all my regulars. It was only when my couple with the dog stopped coming by that I grew desolate and lost my interest in the others and was confined to looking out always for them.

And then at last, after my long vigil, they came back. At least he came back, on his own, leading the dog. I should say I could be certain it was him, only because of the dog, who was such a striking dog. It had to be the same dog, no question. But the young man was changed. I saw at once, being trained to hair, that his had lost its curl and had deepened in colour. And he was leaner in his clothes, slender even – yes, slender. And shorter – though I'm prepared to admit that could be a trick of his leaner outline, the proportions altered. Naturally, without her, he would be changed. But the strange thing was he did not seem lonely, his step was brisk as if he had something to do, or to go to, somewhere later on.

Well, she was away, I concluded. Yes, she would be in the country, visiting her family. A family member had taken sick. Something pressing had called her away, something unavoidable. For he was all her pleasure and all her thoughts ...

But I never was to see her again. Only him, and he always brisk and always cheerful. I had no explanation for it.

'Has he her under the floorboards?' said my fiancé with a laugh.

I watched him, the young man I mean, with increasing anxiety after that. Nothing to do with the floorboards remark, of course, I didn't take that seriously. My fiancé was watching too much television and starving his imagination with its boring plots. No, because of the conviction that was forming in my mind.

Day by day it was plainer to me. The alterations in his appearance that made him so different to his former self and yet made him so weirdly familiar. Once recognised such insights cannot be put aside again. The fact was, you see, he had come to resemble her. Yes, my realisation was that he had become his girlfriend. While remaining also himself.

Oh my god, I almost missed him there, thinking too much and not keeping my eye on the street ... Here he comes now, that inward but cheerful expression on his girlish – yes, girlish – face. As if absorbed in a self-communing, carrying on a harmonious conversation with himself. And the dog comes to a halt at the railings as it generally does and pulls him towards me so I can see him full on. Though there's no way he can see me of course, through the perfectly-adjusted slatted blinds. I couldn't bear for him to think himself watched and adopt another route, I couldn't bear it. I've taken every precaution.

Already I've absorbed the burgundy-striped jeans he's wearing that used to be hers. But of what significance are the jeans I tell myself firmly. I do not jump easily to conclusions. Anyone can pull on a pair of jeans that happen to be lying on the floor, they are only material – and then I see the really significant thing. Calm, unseeing, his gaze meets mine. And I see that his eyes are no longer pellucid, nor pale. Yes, they are muddied water, tan as milky tea when the cup is half empty and gone too cold ...

That was some time ago. It seems so long ago. Once more he – or they, to be exact – departed my sight. Day by day I watched, waited, four to five. Evening after evening, seven to eight ... Watching with a luxuriant frankness and in better comfort since my fiancé is rarely at home these days. His work, the pub, the match, any old excuse will do – he's fallen into all those distractions, like so many men before him. I'm beginning to fear that avenue is closing off to me. He's a disappointment. But I do miss the varying expressions of his face.

Yesterday he came in to pick up something or other he wanted but unfortunately it was at a time when I have to be at my keenest. He went off again without as much as a word. Some of it my fault? A kind of infidelity? I can see he could say that.

Twenty after four now. It's a relief, I must say, not to have to think about his tea and to be able to wait in peace. The couch is really perfectly placed since I got the bay window in. I have a much finer view to the right and the left. I get the full panorama now, both ways. The last straw, my fiancé called it. 'This is the last straw.' Anger overcame the wary in him. But the bay is worth it.

The leaves on the cherry tree falling, swirling to left and right as they are carried on the wind. Can they be falling, and so soon? Another year falling, winding – yes, wind-ing down – and again nothing decided, once more nothing accomplished ... Another year closer to the final separation, the final solitude. But I won't give up hope. Hang on, oh, ohmygod can you believe it ... He's coming – they're coming ...

I tell you, just turned the corner, walking fast, too fast. Nearly a trot. But wait, it can't be, where's the dog? And yet it has to be. But the dog not with them, what can that mean? The gait, the swinging hair, as familiar to me as ... Is that only the wind catching it, the chilly beams of sunlight, illuminating ... No, no, it's definitely greyed, the hair is greying ... It's like ... yes, it's the dog's coat ... brindled, spotted. Weird designer kind of hair. He's coming closer, stopping ...

Watches ... peers at the ground ... and then dashes on, like, like ... And he's snacking away from a packet he holds in his hands. Short stubby hands. Funny, I never thought of them eating, never thought of them doing anything boring like domestic ... And he's right by the railings, comes to a sudden halt ... tugs at a biscuit. It's a Jacob's Cracker. Throws it between his teeth, fine big teeth ... He's peering in, eager ... You could swear he's looking directly at ... Despite myself I shrink back, he shouldn't see, I should not let him know ... But oh, I want him to know, want them ...

Two bites and he has the biscuit swallowed. I watch his face, see it's plumping up, rounding out ... And there he is off again, oh, too soon, swinging down the street as if he's sniffing the air, cheerful and brisk and eager as ... as ... I never thought they could, I never imagined ... Three in one. Oh, I never thought ...

Mary O'Donnell

A Genuine Woman

The evening before our lives were almost destroyed with shock I went into the garden and leant over the limestone wall. I must have been quite still for some minutes, my thoughts drifting, for quite suddenly the fox appeared. From the corner of my eye I glimpsed it. Then I turned and all I got was an aftermath of orange, rust, the streak of his foxiness left imprinted on the eye.

It's strange the things you remember. Not the event itself that connected us to the war. That doesn't come first, although it should, God knows it should. Often, it's the fox I see when I think of that day, because I also glimpsed one at daybreak, only two days later, as I stood at the landing window with Sean's old copybook in my hand, as I read and re-read his records: *Bag for Season 1939–40*. It's the fox I still see when I try to keep hold of myself after what happened, to keep the thing in my heart. It's not as if Mike doesn't know. I believe he does, that he tolerates it, tolerates my struggle with my own heart.

On Sundays Sean would sometimes take his gun out. He showed

me his log-book the day before he died, and for some reason which I cannot recall left it behind him in the kitchen, everything written up in his square handwriting, a month by month and season by season account, dated and totted up to show the total bag for any season. For example, I know that in the first week of February that year he shot seven rabbits, two pigeons, two duck, five teal and four snipe. His total bag for that month came to thirty-three.

'Ah Kate, sure it's me you should've married!' Sean would tease me.

'You must be joking, boy!' I'd scoff, smiling in spite of myself, knowing what would come next.

'I might not be much, I know that ...'

That bit always upset me. Maybe he was smart, running himself down like that, or maybe he was truly humble. I think he was humble, quite different from Mike, who, when I thought about it, had had everything at his beck and call.

Mike was always coddled. Adored by all, his mother and father, and the aunt and uncle that reared him. Loaned at the age of two to the aunt for a few weeks, sent the few miles down the road to their farm, before long he had them charmed. Just like he charmed me later on. His parents, who had children of their own, left him there. An act of compassion, you might say. Whatever way they loved him, it filled him with ideas and plans and interests. Now he is the creamery manager at the Shelburne Co-Operative Society, Campile, and I am his wife. The aunt frowned on me. Still does. Not good enough. A dairymaid that spent her days whacking butter after the churning, shaping and squaring the pound and half-pound with the butter-clappers till it fitted the waxy paper. The ridges of the clappers had to be scrubbed till they were sterile.

'Sterility is everything! Everything!' Mike would roar at us girls, terrified of bacteria.

But he was a gentleman, I'll say that for him. That continued after the wedding too. When first I began to notice his interest in me, I was struck by his nervousness. He was almost cold. Almost. He can look very strict when he's not sure of his ground. Fear makes him himself more erect than ever, the shoulders stiffen and his face is like a mask, the long hollows below his cheekbones full of shadows and the darkness which hints at where he shaves.

But then he began to consult me about things that were unnecessary and obvious to anyone but an imbecile. He would point out different aspects of the new machinery in the dairy, running his hand over the tinned copper piping, or along the side of the great vats. Everything in our working lives was milky. The smell of it, the froth of it as it rose in the vats when the farmers delivered, then the other smell that came when it was heated, for separation, to one hundred and ten degrees Fahrenheit. When the cream came off, it in turn was pasteurised to one hundred and ninety degrees Fahrenheit. The slops, the skim went back to the farmers for whatever use they wished. The dairy had a biscuity, safe odour, almost of the breast, except nicer and sweeter, and there was maybe a thousand gallons of the stuff.

I wore a new suit for our wedding, dark green wool with a black velvet collar and velvet trimming along the edges. The buttons were in a lighter green, some kind of glassy stuff. He insisted on going to Dublin to choose the best he could afford. The wedding was reported in the local newspaper, ending with the words: *The happy couple are spending their honeymoon touring the West of Ireland.* We stayed in The Old Ground Hotel, Ennis, then we visited the Burren. A strange place, compared to what we were used to. I could not feel safe on those great plains of stone, no matter what unusual flowers and weeds grow there. The Cliffs of Moher terrified me. Mike became impatient with me, because

I refused to stand up in the huge gales that blew that day. If the truth be told, I often felt lonely on my honeymoon. The only place I warmed to was a coral strand in Connamara, one evening as the sun turned the restless waters of the Atlantic to floating fires, and the mountains behind us were foxlike in colour.

Afterwards, Mike thought of everything. He never wanted me to be worn out having children year after year, like his own mother before him. Ours were never to be reared with an aunt or uncle, no matter how kindly. So children we had. Two sons. Then no more children. He saw to that on his one and only trip to London. On his return, they didn't check his luggage at Customs. It is one of those things that still fills me with mirth, to think of those grim-faced customs officers watching out for dirty books and pictures and preventatives of any kind. The things he took home to Campile proved useful enough, once we understood how to use them. The book, which was written by a woman called Mrs Marie Stopes, explained everything. These items I kept in the mahogany tallboy, in a special drawer with a lock on it, for my woman's things, (where I also keep Sean's copybook now). Mike thought that the best thing, that I would have recourse to the preventatives when and as I thought necessary. He was not, in spite of the care that he took to provide the things that helped us in matters of love, a great initiator. That was left up to me. Still and all, Mr DeValera up in Dublin city was well and truly foxed, hell mend him!

When the boys were six and four, Sean Flynn began to bring our milk up the road to the house in a bucket, the froth still on the top and it still warm from the cow. I pasteurised it my own way, by boiling it first, then leaving it to cool. When it had cooled, the crinkled skin, which we all hated, could be scooped off.

I was nicely settled in my married life, no worries of a material kind. On Sundays Mike's mother and aunt would sometimes visit us, bringing flowers for me and sweets for the children. I hated those afternoons, stifling they were, with lots of talk about who was sick and who had just died. Of course, the old people, being nearer to death than most of us, liked to dwell on it. It wasn't so bad when Mike's uncle came too. He had an eye for the women, it was said. Either way, he liked me, and he liked the tea I made, strong and black. He would hug me longer than necessary when he arrived and when he went. He meant no harm. I did not receive such a lot of hugs when I was a child, and took what affections he gave. Sometimes Mike and I and the boys would take a drive in the motorcar, in and around the Black Stairs Mountains, uphill and down dale, always with our camera at the ready.

During the week when Sean called, he and I would get to talking, and could we laugh! That's part of the trouble between men and women. As soon as you can laugh together, there's a chance you'll grow close. At that time, it was no more than laughter. He'd tell me funny stories about the ones down in the dairy, or how Mike wouldn't let Pat the Wheels, one of the Wheels Lynches, on account of all the cartwheels lying around their farm, deliver milk until he learnt how to scald his churns properly. Mike was a devil, he was like something possessed when he started on that. But Sean made it sound a hoot, and even though I was laughing at Mike, we both were, we didn't mean it unkindly. 'You can't imagine what class of craytures would be in that milk, Pat,' Sean would imitate Mike, pulling himself up to his full height, 'Craytures that could kill us all and have the creamery shut down by the men in Dublin,' he'd carry on, 'things that'd have you rolling on the floor with the pain in your gut. Then where'd we be at all, at all? Peritonitis is it? Is that what we want?'

Sean was small, yet somehow he could do Mike to a T, and I'd be falling around the place with laughter, burying my face in my apron.

'And then,' says Sean, gripping my forearm to hold my attention even more, 'and then Pat, he says like, all stammery, "Ye mean … ye mean … enough to kill a man?" and your good husband he says nothin' at all, just stands there tellin' it with his eyes, by gob but you should see him Kate!'

Sometimes I stopped the laughing game before it ran its full course. If the children were up the fields Sean could spend half the morning with me. I'd carry on as usual, doing everything I would normally do – bread in the oven, eggs gathered – the only difference being that I was aware of Sean. Sometimes he brought a couple of rabbits, shot earlier in the day, and we'd skin them together. Eventually, I let him do it himself. Skinning creatures has never appealed to me, even though, properly done, it peels off like a little grey jumper. Sometimes he helped me scrub the bedsheets, up and down with the brush on the washboard.

'That's enough now Sean,' I'd say, doing my best to be sensible.

'Ah go on would you Kate, sure what harm? Can't I give you a hand now and then?'

'No harm. But still.'

'Still what?'

I could never answer that. I did not want to say the words. But then, one day I did.

'You're a single man.'

'More's the pity,' he said, smiling slowly at me then.

'You know how I'm fixed,' I said, expecting him to take notice.

'Not a one cares. Sure they think I'm a featherhead. An aul fella with one aul gun and no thoughts of an'thin' beyond his station.'

I turned my back then. I did not want him to see me blush. I was suddenly happy, a bit afraid too, but mostly happy. Perhaps something happens to us in spring. That spring I was like a mad thing, full of the happiness that came from talking to Sean. His eyes were bright blue, with a dark scar above one eyebrow where he fell on glass as a child. He had a headful of curly hair, very little grey for his age, all his own teeth too. I used to watch as he moved around the kitchen, talking away about this one and that one. The hair curled lightly on his forearms, down to the backs of his hands, which were very long and strong. A lifetime's labouring had shaped them.

When Mike and I went to the pictures one night in Waterford, I came out of the cinema with my head full of notions. I could not help it. As Mike tucked the rug around my knees and ankles before he cranked up the motorcar, my thoughts whirled inside my head. The film, which was called *Gone with the Wind*, was in Technicolor. Oh, the colour of the ladies' dresses and Scarlett O'Hara's in particular. I will never forget it, all the dancing and laughter, the big talk from very handsome men. It was the most beautiful film I have ever seen, all of us there trying not to cry, pretending that cigarette smoke had got in our eyes. You could hear a pin drop at two bits in particular. The first was when Melanie died, the other was when Rhett Butler forced himself over Scarlett's body and we all waited, dying to see whether she would enjoy that or reject him because of it. Then there were the bits when he just kissed her, or the way she would look up at him. I also enjoyed the part when she flaunted herself before him and all of society, in a dress made out of old velvet curtains. Yet as Mike let the brake off the motorcar and we drove away, all he could say was 'Well, that's that.' I was so full of something unspeakable that I did not dare answer in case I screamed. At times like that, Mike could fill my heart with disappointment, anger too. Even though he did not mean it, even though he was a good man, the best of men, something began to churn in me. I thought of the old butter churns still used in the country beyond the creamery, and even the big creamery churns, turning and turning until the liquid separated from the lumpy bits, and I saw the bits of my own life separating, some of them drifting and sticking in shapes beyond my control, while the thinner bits of me, or the bits that seemed thin and of no consequence, just slopped there in unwanted pools.

Two nights later, Sean went to the pictures by himself. The day after, he came up to me as usual, with the bucket of milk from the dairy. He looked bashful, quiet in himself. Full well I knew what was on his mind though we'd said nothing to one another. He opened a packet of cigarettes, lit one slowly, sucked in hard, keeping his eyes down as he did so. Only as he breathed out did he look at me.

'Which bit did you like the best?'

His eyes stayed on my face. I felt myself blush horrid hot, so much that I wanted to run from the kitchen. Quickly, I turned and dragged a bag of spuds from beneath the sink, fired them into a basin. I took a knife and began to peel like blazes. The sound of the peeling had its own quick rhythm, because although I did not mean it to, the blade of the knife kept hitting off the blue enamel edge of the basin. They were the cleanest spuds you ever did see by the time they reached the saucepan.

'Did you hear me, *a stoirin*? Which bit?'

I kept my head turned from him, and I answered.

'The bit where Ashley and Melanie run towards one another. When he comes back from war.'

It's true I enjoyed that part, but not as much as some other parts.

'Have you stars in your eyes today, then?' he enquired softly from where he stood, with his back to the range. I glanced over my shoulder at him, then turned away again. His look was amused, gentle. He was well able to tease just then, knowing that, somehow, he had the upper hand. Everything was quiet at that moment, save for the soughing wind in the apple branches, and a couple of starlings fighting over a scrap of bacon fat on the window ledge.

'Put some coal on that range for me, would you Sean?' I called back over my shoulder with a light laugh.

He futhered with the lid for a while before he got it opened, then lifted the copper scuttle. As the coal tumbled in with a loud grating, black smoke puffed out into the kitchen, so that we were both coughing a bit. He replaced the lid quickly. But he didn't let up.

'You have stars in your eyes, haven't you?' he said again, more teasingly, as if he was insisting on something.

This time I just coughed by way of avoiding an answer. I marched out of the kitchen and down to the hen house. I wasted little time picking my bird, tucked her under my arm and marched back up the garden towards the kitchen. Sean was watching from over the half door. There was uproar among the hens, as if they knew what was coming. The rooks were circling the yard as usual, cawing and screeching. Two magpies cackled on the plum trees, scattering the white blossom in little darts and spirals.

'I'll give you stars in the eyes, Sean Flynn!' I took the chicken and wrung its neck. I was good at that. Swift and clean. The birds hardly knew they were dead. This one didn't even squawk.

I did not see Sean until the following week. Something had changed between us. Perhaps we had declared ourselves. I was truly agitated by the prospect of his return. I knew he would come back, wanted him to. Delivering our daily milk was, after all, one of his jobs.

My eyes wandered restlessly as I worked, drawn always to whatever was happening outside the window, whether I was in the kitchen or the parlour, or in the bedrooms, or indeed in the bathroom where Mike spent so much time splashing and preening himself every morning. (Small wonder the boys still brought chamber pots to their bedrooms. He wouldn't let anybody near the bathroom in the morning, until he was well and truly finished. He had leathers and razors galore, nose-clippers and ear-clippers, blades and cutting implements for dealing with every kind of hair under the sun, no matter where it was located. Me, I never bothered much with the solitary hair that sprang from a small mole above my lip. Sometimes I cut it, but it didn't worry me. For some reason, the few hairs I once had on my bosoms fell away after the boys were born. Everything else is as nature intended.)

But that spring I was full of nervous strength. Strength, that was it. I was so bursting with it I could have mown my way through a field of ripe corn, or danced all night, had I the chance, or done things which I dare not commit to paper. Instead I kept the house clean. I was busier than ever. I made myself so. Some of the rooms in the house I have never liked, the ones that are too dark, or which show the old-fashioned taste of the previous manager's wife. A drab soul, she must have been. But our bedroom, with the shining brass bed and a creamy-white bolster with lace edging, the dressing-table on which I keep brushes, one ivory comb, some face-cream and a bottle of perfume, is a delicious place. I enjoy being a wife, in spite of all. The wifely things, the habits and touches that go with my station, bring ease and civility and peace. The view from that bedroom window always pleased me, falling down the hill from the back of the house towards the big stream, and beyond that again the field with the beech trees and the sweet beech nuts that I gorged myself on when I was expecting both children.

One day I made myself stop the mad cleaning and polishing. The youngest child was with me, the other boy at school. I treasured the last few months of my baby boy's true freedom. In September, he would be gone from me, to the schoolroom, to rules and regulations, so that he could learn to read and write and count and become a proper little Irishman during Mr DeValera's Emergency. Makes my heart ache still, to think of it. But there we were, and me playing with him in the front garden. I had the box camera. I settled the child on top of one of the pillars by the gate, all ready to take a photograph. He still wore his little winter boots and the grey socks Mike's aunt liked to knit. Terrible things to look at, but warm.

'Now, *mo pheata*,' I coaxed, 'You give me that big smile of yours, the one your Mammy loves so well.'

He knew how to charm, little man that he was. My heart filled with joy when he smiled and I looked down into the camera, transfixed by his broad grin and the small white teeth as he pulled his face wide just to please me.

'Ah, there's the good boy, the best boy ever!' I crooned for a moment afterwards, scooping him off the pillar and into my arms. But this is the strange thing. I knew full well that my joy was not entirely for my son. I knew that my heart soared like a lark for Sean Flynn, who had just turned in the gate as I lifted the child down. I've heard of dentists who give laughing gas to their patients. Well, I imagine that if I had had laughing gas it might have felt as good as what ran through me just then. It wasn't that I laughed out loud. This was something within me, a spring in some secret mossy place that nobody before has ever discovered. I wanted to shout about it, to tell everyone, to let the spring overflow and make its way to the unknown, wild, beautiful ocean where I could dream and drown with the joy of it all. And I wonder if there's a difference between dreaming and drowning?

Sean was taken by surprise, seeing me there. Immediately, he put the bucket down on the gravel path, beside the polleny shrubs that tumbled around, never pruned when they should be.

'May I take a picture of you? May I? I'd like to, if I may,' he said, suddenly more polite and correct in his English than I had ever heard him before.

I was wearing a big hat that day, and a new blue dress from Switzers of Dublin, and little cream leather shoes with fine double straps and the very latest heels.

'Yes,' was all I said.

'You look a picture anyway, did you know that?' he said then.

'Thank you,' I managed to reply.

'Good enough to ate, *a stoirin*.'

I could smell him. A clean sweat smell, I saw it moist on his neck as he craned sideways to see where he would take the photograph. Little did he know what torments his neck and throat were to me.

'Now.'

'Now what? I haven't got all day,' I began, then stopped myself. I can always sound more severe than I mean to.

'Ah don't be like that,' he said.

'Like what?'

'Bossy. Mike's wife.'

'But that's what I am.'

'And my friend,' he answered, his gaze firm.

It took ages for him to decide where to put me. First he set me beside the sundial at the centre of the lawn, positioning me this way and that, with my head slightly raised. Then he changed his mind and set me standing beneath the lilac tree, looking away into the distance, as if I was thinking of something and not in the least aware that my picture was being taken.

'You're very fussy,' I ventured to comment, watching him now as he took stock of the situation in a way I had never before seen.

'A very important piece of technology, this,' he said seriously, 'and the photographin' of a lady like yourself should be done proper.'

In the end he made me go back to the sundial, leaning one elbow on the dial itself. Just as I settled myself, Pat the Wheels Lynch went by with his donkey and cart and two churns. He took a good gander in, his two eyes glued to the little scene in the garden. Even if the other business with the Germans had not happened, I was done for and I knew it. Next thing Pat would be down at the crossroads shop filling Mrs Sullivan and her nosey daughter Mary in on the sight he had beheld. But I did not care.

'Now, turn towards me, no, no, look – wouldja folly me hand! Look where me hand is pointin',' he ordered. I did what I was told too, calm in those few moments when he held the shape of me in a little square bit of the box. It wasn't that he was looking *at* me, so much as *into* that place called the soul, which the priesteens around the county so like to talk about, but with little understanding.

Later, when the pictures came back from the chemist's in New Ross, Mike hardly looked at the ones of me, though he took great care examining the child's. It wasn't that he was indifferent, so much as remiss. That happens, even with the best of husbands. Because they trust their wives, they forget that trust is not always to be guaranteed. Not long after that day, Sean kissed me. It was an awkward, short kiss, as if he was terrified, which he was, but I held on to him when the kiss had ended, because with that kiss, he entered a part of me that no one had ever before entered. I put my arms around him and hugged him very carefully, so that he would know I welcomed him. 'There now,' I whispered, 'it's all right, hush now ...'

There was a new sadness in his face that day as he left, as if he had been disturbed. Perhaps his feelings were in uproar like my own, raided with desire as if something from outside our lives had dropped on the pair of us.

I still cannot believe what happened next. No, that is not true. But it confounds me. That summer was like any other until August, the days long, the fields and hedges and trees ripe. Meadowsweet, purple vetch, nettles, yarrow, the barley waving like a pale yellow sea. Sean and I whiled away many an hour together.

According to his records, which I slip from the drawer every so often, Sean bagged three rabbits in August, four duck and three teal. The previous August, he had bagged thirty rabbits, three pigeon, two duck and three teal. He shot no duck the December before, but six snipe, three woodcocks and twelve rabbits.

I will never know what notion took him that he stayed so long at the creamery restaurant that day. Probably to chat to the girls. What I remember is the whine, unlike anything I have ever heard before, getting louder and louder, so that we all knew it was not a fire siren, but something else, something deadly. The ferocious sound fell to its awful conclusion, thunder to cap all thunders, an earthquake sound because it seemed as if the whole world had been split asunder, a devilish, evil, roaring thing that shook us in our bones and souls. I was in the hen house just then. The children screamed with fright from further up the garden, then raced down to me and clung to my legs. I could feel their bodies atremble, even though my own legs went weak as water. People everywhere stopped what they were doing. I crossed my chest without thinking.

That evening, when the worst was known, I could hardly stand for the weeping, so that Mike had to put the two boys to bed. I did not care. *The Irish Independent* carried a full account the following morning, although I did not read it for a week or more.

Three girls – two of them sisters – and one man were killed and others were injured when the creamery in which they were working at Campile, Co. Wexford, was wrecked yesterday afternoon when a German aircraft dropped bombs in Campile, Ballynitty, Bannow and Duncormick. The dead girls are: Mary Kate Hoare, aged 35, and her sister, Catherine Hoare (25) of Bannow, and Kathleen Kenny (25) of Tacumshin. Mr Sean Flynn (44) of Campile, also died in the incident. They were at work in the restaurant of the Shelburne Co-operative Agricultural Society Ltd, when it was struck by a bomb and reduced to ruins. The bodies were buried beneath the debris and were dead when extricated ...

Rumours spread, of course. People said that Shelburne Creamery butter-wrappers had been found in Dunkirk and that the Germans must have thought it was a big source of butter to Britain. Others said the German pilot had lost his way, or that he was getting rid of his load before returning to base.

It is no secret that I loved Sean Flynn. Mike knows it too, and has not been hard on me on account of it. Half the neighbourhood had been gabbing about us for a long time anyway. I imagine however, that none of them today lie awake at night thinking about me and my little problems. They have enough of their own.

When I think back to before that time, I see my life running along smoothly, even though things often perplexed me. But I was happier than I knew. Everything was normal and ordinary, just as it is again. The ordinariness is not so good now. Nowadays, I live true to everything and everyone. I am what some might call genuine. I do not give a hoot for being genuine, not since Sean died. Through him I understood that surface sincerity was not everything; that sincerity has an underbelly that it is not always possible to be true to. Most people avoid that tender spot. It is the difference between a lake and the ocean. Both are water, but I would choose the ocean any day, for its greatness, its solid will. Nothing contains the ocean, only gravity.

We never did more than kiss.

Cherry Smyth

Walkmans, Watches and Chains

There was very little furniture in the room as if someone had forgotten to finish putting things in it or was thinking about moving away. There were no cushions on the green vinyl settee, no ornaments on the shelves. I knew then that he wasn't married. There was a picture of the sea arch at the White Rocks above the mantelpiece. And some photographs.

'Who's that?' I said.

'That's a photo of my wee niece,' he said. 'A school photo.'

I remember thinking he was OK if he had a niece, his own people. I remember feeling that I was the thing that finished the room.

'You have lovely hair,' he said.

I'd heard that before. But not the way he said it. He said it as though he wanted it for himself, the way another girl would. 'I'm growing it till I can sit on it.'

'It must keep you warm at night,' he said.

I'd never thought of it. The word 'warm' rubbed up against 'at night' and made a buzz in the room I'd been listening out for. His bungalow was in a crescent that used to be a field and I could hear other children playing on the green circle of new grass in front of the houses, as if they were in another part of his house. Most of the crescent still had 'For Sale' signs. There was little traffic up there, which is why we used to race around it on our bikes and roller skates. It had nice smooth tarmac that turned off into each driveway like petals on a black flower.

'So, the bike?' I said.

He'd been putting up a bird table on his lawn and had offered to fix my puncture. The bike was in the hallway. I talked to it like it was a live person, half-bike, half-boy. It wasn't like going in there on my own, having my bike.

'Let me give your hair a brush first,' he said. 'A hundred strokes.'

'That's alright,' I said. I tidied my hair-band and flicked my hair off my shoulders. The blush fell around my neck.

'I can make it more lovely,' he said. 'Silky-shiny.'

He got up and took a hairbrush from the shelf. It was an old-fashioned one with yellow bristles and flowers pressed under the glass. It made me sad for him because it was some lady's, and she was probably dead. He signalled with it and I took a step towards him and placed my feet together. He stood behind me and began to brush my hair. I looked at the fireplace rug and concentrated on where sparks had burnt little black holes in the pattern.

Then he sat down and pulled me between his knees. He kept brushing and strands of hair floated up to follow the brush, light with static. I love people playing with my hair. My eyes go heavy, my scalp extra alive. I didn't mind him doing it. John. At first his knees didn't touch my thighs. And then they did. He had scratchy trousers and I could feel them itching my skin. I thought he wouldn't notice if I moved away, as though my hair could stay under the brush and I could slip out and take my bike and push off down the hill. When I fidgeted, he told me to keep still. All the time I was aware that I shouldn't be in his front room, but the sense that something would happen held me there, as if I had to stay and prove I was right. I saw myself asleep on his couch with my hair covering my body. It was not a premonition that frightened me – it was mine, not his, but he had made me dream it. I grew up the minute I saw it.

Then I realised he was stroking my hair with his hands, not the brush, flattening his palms down it, like you would pet an animal. I didn't budge because I didn't want him to stop. His hands moved down my back, over my skirt, as if my hair was long enough to sit on, as if I had a mane all down my body. I was part-girl, part-pony, drifting in sand-hills that crumbled like cake under my feet. I was paddling, his hands the water's edge.

'Right, that's enough,' he said and he clapped his hands, moved me forward and stood up. 'Let's see to this bicycle.'

I remember him tipping the bike upside down and getting out his spanners and a bowl of water. He got me to kneel down and watch for bubbles hissing from the inner tube. The mood that swam in the room before was gone, professionally put away. It reminded me of when Mr Wilson made a mistake on the board which some pupil noticed and he'd fumble and let his other man, the home man, slip out, then he'd become a real teacher again, certain and clean at the edges. So it was clear why John didn't look at me when he chalked the puncture, glued on the patch and held it in place. He was keeping that man who wanted my hair tucked in behind his face. He put the tyre back on the wheel, pumped it up and righted the bike.

'Now skedaddle,' he said, swinging open the front door. 'And don't let me catch you up round here again.'

His voice was the minister's voice. Out of breath and too loud. He was speaking to the outside. He looked ugly. The effort of not liking me bunched up his features. I hadn't noticed his looks before that. He was old. With combed-back grey and black hair.

As I left, I noticed his car. A white Austin. And I knew, like you know when you're about to fall off your bike riding downhill, that I would go for a spin in that car some afternoon, up to the White Rocks maybe.

I cycled home that teatime, my arms strong, guiding my steed, riding out of the saddle to increase my speed. 'Good boy, atta boy,' I said.

I wasn't sure what was going to happen next. I felt as though hidden cameras were making a film and the next scene would come if I just turned up in my own life. It made me very calm and very important. I used to walk the mile home from school with my friends, stopping at Cowan's for sweets. I knew nothing would happen, that the next scene would not play until I was on my own. One afternoon I pretended I had to see the drama teacher about the Christmas play and I waited until my friends would have passed the Diamond before I set out. As if we were connected, John drove up along the curb after ten minutes. I imagined him watching the secret flick in his bungalow cinema and knowing exactly when to leave. It made me star in my own world and I shone as I slid into his front seat.

'You look better when you're not in uniform,' was the first thing he said to me. He spoke as though he'd seen me a few minutes, not several weeks, ago. That made me cheeky.

'You'd look better if you were bald.'

He laughed at that. It was the first time I'd heard him laugh and his face lost its tightness about the eyes.

'So, you're a Kojak fan, are you?'

'Yeah, love him.'

'I'm a bit old for that game.'

'Cannon's as old as you,' I said though I wasn't sure. Americans always looked younger than they were.

'Shall we go for a wee run?' he said, as I knew he would.

'Sure,' I said and the movie director told me to put my feet up against the dashboard. John pretended not to notice.

As we drove out of the town he started to sing 'Ticky tacky little boxes,' and it sounded like he could, and that the whole town and all its people bored him and they bored me too.

I kept my hands on my skirt, so it wouldn't rise up my thighs. I knew how and what to show and I was not surprised I knew.

We drove down to the car park by the beach. Behind were the chalk cliffs and further around the headland was the sea arch, where the sea had eaten away at the land. He put on a tape.

'The sea is grand if you don't depend on it,' he said. 'I worked out there. It's a tough business.'

The sea widened as he spoke, a huge screen stretching wider and wider like cinema curtains opening for the big picture. He knew the tide and I was a grain of sand.

'Did you ever nearly drown?' I said.

'Yes,' he said.

'Is it true you see your life flash in front of your eyes?'

'It's true all right. The strong moments. Good and bad. Speeded up and slowed down. You tell yourself you'll be a better person after that.'

'Why did you come back here? Why not Africa or Australia or ... anywhere?'

He turned to me. 'I'll tell you why.' He paused. 'Because Irish girls are the prettiest in the whole world.'

I smiled because I couldn't help it.

He leaned forward and took an Instamatic out of the glove compartment.

'Give me that smile again.'

I went shy. He tilted my chin and took my picture.

'Loosen your tie,' he said. His voice was so low I wasn't certain I'd heard him right.

'My tie?'

'I have something for you.' He didn't move. He was the director. I tugged down the knot and opened the top button of my shirt. He still didn't move. I undid the next button and slid the tie looser.

'That's it.' He snapped another picture. He reached into his jacket pocket and gave me a small jewellery box. I opened it. It was my name in gold letters.

'Let me put it on,' he said.

He dangled the necklace and I held up my hair so that he could fasten it. I was thinking how I could hide it from my mum, who sees through doors. I felt him kiss my neck, quick as a mistake.

'Thanks a lot,' I said, turning my head. My ears were on fire. I didn't like the chain much. My name was spelt wrong.

'It doesn't mean you have to give me anything,' he said. His eyes said the opposite.

'I know.' I looked down at the chain. It hung awkwardly outside my clothes. He straightened the letters. Catherine. My back was stiff against the seat and his thumb played on my shirt as though he'd forgotten to take it away. His fingertips dipped in under the cotton like a fish.

'Do you like it?' he said.

'Yeah, love it.'

I think I might have sighed and looked out of the window. A flock of black and white birds took off, turned swiftly on the wind and became invisible over the water. His hand was gone. The movie was over, the crew vanishing across the waves. 'Come back,' I wanted to shout. 'I'll do that scene again.' But he'd turned the key in the ignition and was reversing out of the parking space.

'You're a nice girl, Cat,' he said.

I smiled. The nickname was his. It meant more than the necklace. It couldn't be spelt wrong.

'Thanks John,' I said.

He began to whistle along to the music. I wanted to touch his cheek. Instead, I dropped the necklace inside my shirt and tightened my tie. When I moved in the seat I felt silky-shiny in my pants. As we came to the outskirts he slowed down to the speed limit. He didn't rake through the gears like my daddy did. He dropped me at the corner of my road where it meets Lark Hill. No one asks the leading lady of the school play anything. I said Miss McGarvey gave me a lift.

When he wasn't there on the road home from school the next Thursday, I dawdled at the Diamond, ate two Crunchies that spiked my tongue, made every passing white car his. That Saturday, I rode my bike up to Seaview Crescent. I circled on the tarmac, one eye on the blank windows of John's bungalow. His car was in the drive. I sailed past, willing the film to start. Nothing. The car was my ally. It too, waited. Missed him. I memorised the number. I circled again, curving nearer to his house. Then I saw him at the window watching me. I kept cycling, standing on the pedals, showing my command of the handlebars. Then he was gone. If only I could somersault off the bike, bang my head, have him carry me inside, lay me on the couch, put a cold flannel on my brow, tidy my hair. Was that the next scene? Look, no hands! I cruised, wobbled and almost toppled, but I lost my nerve and grabbed for the handlebars. Then I heard it. Two notes of a whistle like you'd call for a dog. He was standing in the garage. I pedalled in. He pulled down the door.

My chest was thumping like sick gathered there ready to come up. I let the bike fall. He held me up against him. My arms went round him. His heart beat in my face. I didn't want more than that, to be hugged, to feel my smallness against him, to know everything he'd known about the town, the women, the men, lovers, movie stars. I knew that if he kissed me I would puke.

He didn't kiss me, but he said things in my ear. He said my name, my full name as if he'd forgotten his name for me. He said he had something special for me, his mother's watch, he'd like to give me as a present. He pulled down my shorts and pushed a finger into my pants and into somewhere I didn't know I had. He was breathing fast and his finger was rough, like a finger that says, 'come here' for punishment, curling and uncurling. He undid his zipper with his other hand. If I was good, he said, he'd get me a Walkman. Would I like that? he said. The garage was too dim to see his face or for him to see mine, and the fear that must have widened it like an empty screen. I struggled to get away, but the finger kept curling, 'here, here' and his words burned in my ear like a creature in a seashell winding in deeper and deeper.

He pushed me down to my knees and something bumped my temple. It felt like a toddler's arm. I was confused, like there was another person there. I started to shout, 'Stop. Please, John. No!' But the arm was a stump and he wedged it into my mouth so no sound could get out. He squeezed the back of my head and moved me back and forth on his pullie. There was a smell of petrol and dead mice. He pushed against the back of my throat, speeding up and slowing down. He didn't whistle or sing. He peed in my mouth and groaned. Then he stopped. I was crying and my body was quaking. I spat him out of my mouth.

'I'm sorry Cat,' he said. 'I'm sorry that had to happen.' He was half-sobbing. He stroked my hair with heavy, blind hands. I ducked and stumbled away from him. I felt among the garden tools for my bike. I wanted to boke. I wanted to boke on my own, away from his smell.

'*Shh* now,' he said, taking my arm. I kicked against him. 'Go easy now, girl.'

'You're a dirty disgusting pig,' I said. The corners of my mouth were sore when I screamed. 'Let me out of here.'

He shook my shoulders, steadied me.

'I'll let you go, just calm yourself. Calm yourself.'

'I'm going to die. I can't breathe.' I gulped at the stale, grass-clipping air. I choked and made myself choke more. He had taken away the air, the light. He panicked and opened the door into the kitchen. I walked into the day as if I was folded down the middle. He led me to the bathroom and left me there. I didn't look in the mirror. I ran the hot tap till it steamed and then I threw the water up over my face and into my mouth. My hands were tiny, my fingers bird bones and the water scattered everywhere. I rinsed and spat. I chewed some toothpaste. I heard his front door open and close. I went to the hall. I could see outside. He had leant my bike against the wall. The green where I'd been cycling was still lit gold by the sun. I wanted to see my mummy. Everyone would believe the star of the school play.

I stepped across the grass. There was a long T-shadow from the bird table and my shadow crossed it and bent in behind me like a dark leak. The bike looked too small. I was afraid I wouldn't remember how to ride it. I pushed the bike along the pavement where Mill Lane used to be, and blackberries and no proper road. Everyone would know. The whole school. The whole audience. There were smudges of grease on my knees. I stopped and rubbed them with spittle but they smeared more. Tim Dalzell from school was ahead on the pavement. I pulled my face into shape, tucked my hair behind my ears. I got on the bike to pass him quicker. He said hi. I said hello but nothing came out. I wavered, then I spun down the hill not knowing if I could stop at the bottom.

Catherine Dunne

Moving On

What Anthony and I used to call his 'Moses sandals' were eventually recovered three miles from our house, at the south end of the beach.

The beige leather was scratched and battered. Seaweed had become entangled in each of the silvery buckles, but otherwise they were unchanged. They washed up one after the other, twenty-four hours apart.

Waiting on the second one acquired an eerie quality, as though the sandal would struggle home with Anthony attached, his hair streaming, eyes blazing, mouth formed around a lopsided grin – in short, just as I was used to seeing him when work exercised its compulsion. Instead, the second sandal arrived alone on the rocky foam, jostling its way home quietly, apologetically.

Even then, I wasn't ready to acknowledge the truth which that sandal brought with it. I conceded that it knew something I didn't. That was all. The police were grave, uneasily polite. We were an oddity, Anthony and I: the fifty-year-old Englishman, the thirty-year-old Irishwoman with her pale, small baby – although those around us had never learned to distinguish our nationalities. Irish? English? What was the difference? What did it matter? Our pale skin was whiter than any seen on the island, all those years ago. Our peppered freckles, our shared language, our foreignness: these things shrugged us into sameness.

At least, that seemed to be Anthony's view. I always thought – have always known – it was something deeper than that. Often, when I went to the market, there was a peculiar charged silence as I went from stall to stall. In the still blue heat of the morning I'd point out my purchases of the day: huge, misshapen tomatoes, glossy peppers, blocks of creamy feta in its watery liquid. On a couple of occasions, back in the early days following our arrival, I'd attempt the few Greek words that Mama Kalanaikas had tried to teach me. But I gave up. The stallholder would open his folded arms as though to embrace me, but instead would show me, again and again, the spread palms of his incomprehension. Market mornings always brought with them that haze of resentful curiosity. It was worse when Anthony accompanied me – this impatient, paint-spattered man encroaching on women's business.

'Don't linger so, Martha,' he'd sigh. 'Just pay up and leave.'

I'd pack the goods away hurriedly, careful not to bruise anything. Often, I'd catch the stallholders' eyes as their glance alighted on Anthony's departing back. I needed no translation when one of them, arms folded, leaned deliberately to one side and spat, insolently, into the hot yellow dust. The act shocked me, made me wonder about the hostility of all those men. But Anthony dismissed it.

'It's not your concern,' he said, when I told him what I'd seen. He was using his thumb to texture paint onto canvas. He applied it thickly, then scraped away the excess with his palette knife. Finally, he stood back, judging the effect. I had grown used to this, to waiting, to his not looking at me. 'We're different, that's all, you and I – we don't speak the same language they do.'

At the time, it seemed at least a partly reasonable explanation. We were so obviously foreigners, people who by definition must have had other choices. Perhaps our lives were seen to be mocking theirs. Perhaps our decision to live as locals was regarded as a patronising one.

Anthony had been painting on the terrace that day, the day before he never came home again. He had been working all morning, the large, primed canvas stretched taut against the shaded front wall of our house. He moved constantly, nervously, as he always did, at the start of anything new. He'd lunge to the right, or the left, or swing around and peer at the canvas over his shoulder. Sometimes, he'd dart down the two wooden steps to the beach and look through the frame of his fingers, just as I've seen film directors do in recent years. I used to wonder at the shadowy, violent figures that populated all his work. Once, just after we'd met, I asked him why he never painted *pretty* things. I never asked again.

I can still hear the gritty-sliding sound of his feet on the cool tiles of the terrace. The afternoon heat was fierce, sand like a furnace. I could never grow used to it. I sat on shaded, lumpy cushions and watched over Anna in her tiny cradle. I sucked on fat black olives, their earthy fleshiness restful against my tongue. Anthony's energy often made me feel tired.

Once, about a year before we came to the island, he'd left me alone in Athens for almost a whole winter. That was the longest we'd ever been apart, a week here, perhaps a month there, ever since I was twenty. But he'd always come back. That flat in Athens where we'd hidden away was dark, tiny, its silence seamless. While Anthony travelled, searching for light, for inspiration, for the *transcendent*, I slept. It's strange that I remember nothing from those months, other than the welcome oblivion of sleep. Then, one January morning, I was shaken into wakefulness.

'Come on, Beauty,' he said, his face grinning down into mine. 'We're on the move again.'

Mama Kalanaikas, as we called her, was due to arrive at four, just as the stabbing intensity began to leach out of the sun's rays. Her weekly arrival was as predictable as the afternoon winds which stirred at the same time every day, crumpling the surface of the unforgiving sea below us. We looked forward to her visits, Anthony and I. She, like us, was something of an oddity on the island, albeit a home-grown one. There was, I liked to feel, some kind of complicity between us. Her dark eyes often flashed sympathy, one outsider to another. Her husband had been dead for forty years, yet she never dressed in black as all the other widows did. She was a stern woman, somewhere in her late seventies, skin the colour of old bark. Her earlobes fascinated me. They were thin, the piercings a long vertical slash, heavy with a lifetime's lapis lazuli. Every time I looked at her, the lines and fissures of her face reminded me of spidery pictures of the Nile Delta I had once seen as a child.

'A woman to be respected,' Anthony had said when we'd met her first. '*She's* a woman not to be trifled with.' I can still hear his tone, that casual emphasis.

Mama was courteous, even voluble on occasion. She'd look at Anthony's canvases, perplexed, talk up at him for a moment, and then immediately move to gaze into Anna's cradle. Then she'd turn and pat my arm gently. Next time, she seemed to say. A boy next time. Seven sons, she'd once told me, counting on her fingers. This unspoken female collusion both touched and irritated me. It made me feel guilty – disloyal in some way to Anna. Nevertheless, I welcomed it.

Of course, we none of us understood the *words* the other spoke, but it never mattered. When she'd stand up to leave, Anthony would hand her the discreet envelope containing the rent, almost as an afterthought, as though the purpose of her visits were an altogether different one. We'd had to learn the choreography of those visits, too, almost as another language.

While we awaited her arrival that day, Anthony stopped occasionally to sip at a glass of retsina. He claimed he always worked better in the heady afternoon heat; said that the wine unleashed something in him, some pool of inspiration inaccessible under all other circumstances, at all other times. The wine-bottle was perspiring madly, great big beads of water sliding over its greenish surface. The label had begun to lurch drunkenly just below the neck, scrawled black ink bleeding and blurring into oblivion.

'Are you sure Mama understands that we want to stay on right through the winter?' I asked him. I was tired of always moving on, hiding, shuffling from one inhospitable place to the other. Besides, this was Anna's first home. That had to count for something.

He didn't answer at once.

'Anthony?'

I remember that I had cut great slices of dense white goats cheese that day. It was pleasantly salty, but a little too dry for me. I ate hardly any of it, but Anthony dived into it, as usual. His long fingers plucked at the coarse, yeasty bread that showered crumbs everywhere. The crust was sharp, hard on bare feet. Peasant bread, Anthony used to call it – but with admiration, never with scorn. He always ate distractedly, often with a clutch of brushes in one hand, his fingers mottled with oils and turpentine. He'd pace as he ate, the hand with the brushes swinging in time to his long, impatient step. Up and down the terrace, up and down the beach, always on the move, always on the lookout for something. Occasionally, he would stand abruptly still, staring out to sea. On that day, he stayed on the terrace.

'Please don't question me; don't question what I do,' he said, finally.

I looked up, surprised. 'I wasn't ...'

But he had already turned back to his canvas.

It wasn't Mama Kalanaikas who arrived that afternoon. Instead, it was Nikolai, her eldest son, along with three other men I'd never seen before. The family resemblance was unmistakable. Nikolai came and stood at our bottom step. Anthony waved his invitation to come up onto the terrace.

'Please, please,' he said, 'welcome.'

Nikolai refused with a gesture – swift and curt, strangely at odds with the gold of the sand, the suddenly stirring breeze. I sat back on my cushions, shocked. He inclined his head stiffly in my direction for a moment, without actually looking at me, and then turned his attention to Anthony.

'Mama is ill,' he said softly. 'She send me.'

I jumped up, alarmed. 'Can I help? Does she need anything?'

His eyes flickered. 'We take care good, my mother,' he said quietly.

'Oh, of course, I didn't mean ...'

Anthony silenced me with a glance. He turned gravely to Nikolai. 'We wish your mother a good recovery,' he said slowly. He reached into the little drawer of the tiled side-table and pulled out the weekly envelope. I saw his hand shake. 'Thank you for calling.'

Nikolai bowed. 'We need house, now.'

We both looked at him. His three brothers stood silently on the beach, arms folded. For a wild moment, I felt I had become one of the stallholders in the local market. Nikolai's meaning was perfectly clear, yet I remember that I spread my palms towards him, offering him my incomprehension. At that moment, Anna started to wail. I wanted to go to her, but something kept me anchored there. Standing on the bottom step, I felt caught between my child and a suddenly looming future over which I had no control.

'Our agreement is with your mother,' said Anthony. Then he turned his face and said something else, something I didn't catch. His tone was cold, deliberate, undercut by that jaunty energy I knew so well. Nikolai responded, his words flat and sullen, dangerous edges pushing closer to the surface. *You're dealing with me now. That's the agreement now.*

I couldn't look at Anthony's face.

'It's all Greek to me,' he used to say, cheerfully – or Italian, or Turkish, or French, depending on where we happened to be – priding himself on his inability to master even the simplest sounds. Watching these two men now, I felt the slow drag of familiarity. I knew what happened next. It would happen again, just as surely as it had the last time, and the time before that. I could still see the cool green of the courtyard in Bari, the trickling fountain, the farmer's brown and solemn children.

'Soldi! Soldi!' he'd shouted, jabbing the forefinger of one hand into the palm of the other. Sweat had gathered across his forehead, his shirt was damp. I thought I could smell fear. But Anthony had simply smiled and shaken his head. This canvas, perhaps? Or this one? Maybe a portrait instead?

And afterwards, always the same mantra: 'Come on, Beauty, we're on the move again.'

Anna's wail became a screech. Still I couldn't move. For the first time, Nikolai looked at me, just for a moment. His glance was contemptuous, insolent, yet still suggestive, redolent of invitation. I fled. My cheeks burned as I lifted my small daughter and she latched onto my breast, hungrily. She quieted almost at once. I didn't dare look towards the beach again.

When Anthony stepped up onto the terrace, his face was

tight, pinched with an anger I had seen all too frequently in our ten years together. The anger of another defeat, another scheme unravelling. He put his brushes down very carefully, wiped his long fingers on the front of his shirt.

'I'm going to see Mama,' he said, finally.

I looked at him stupidly, before I understood.

'Don't, please – I don't want to stay here on my own.' I could feel my lower lip tremble, hated the whine in my own voice. I was fearful now, fearful for my own safety and for Anna's.

He smiled suddenly. 'There's nothing to be afraid of, Martha – it's just a misunderstanding. Mama said the house was ours. It was a fair price. She agreed it was a fair price for a year.'

'But you and Nikolai ...'

He interrupted me. 'Never mind Nikolai. It's *Mama's* house – she was very clear about that.'

I remembered. Remembered the afternoon on the beach, just days before Anna's birth, remembered the way Mama had pointed to the house, then back to herself, nodding vigorously all the time. *My* house, she kept saying. Mine. *Mine*. Then she had pulled drachmas out of her skirt pocket, counting and counting until she and Anthony struck a bargain on the rent.

But that wasn't what I wanted to talk about. I tried again.

'Anthony, just now, you and Nikolai ...'

'A misunderstanding, Martha,' he said, curtly. 'Don't go on about it.' He stood over me, rested his hand lightly on the top of Anna's fair head. 'I won't be long,' he said then. 'If Mama's changed her mind, then I want to hear her say it. To my face.'

He was striding along the beach before I could stop him. I wanted to call out, to remind him of folded arms, spreading palms, all the uselessness of words. *It's all Greek to me.* Instead, I watched as he grew smaller, walking away from me towards the south end of the beach.

I clung to Anna. 'I'll keep you safe,' I whispered. 'I'll protect us.'

After that, I'm really not quite sure what happened next, or how long anything took. It has nothing to do with memory: simply that days melded together around that time, hammered into the metal of sameness by the blunt instrument of loss.

When Anthony's body finally washed up on the west coast of the island, it was too far decomposed to ascertain the cause of death. The policeman was very careful to tell me that there were no signs, *no signs at all*, that any violence had 'come to visit Mr Anthony'.

When I left, I took his Moses sandals with me, his brushes and two small canvases. It was all I could carry. The police escorted me to the ferry, accompanied by that same, brittle politeness. They carried my suitcase; I carried Anna. Somehow, I got to Athens again, then Italy, then, finally, home.

I've been thinking about Mama a lot, these days. I realised recently, with some amusement, that I am almost as old now as she was then, although my skin will never acquire the shadings of old bark. I do hope all her sons dealt with her kindly. I don't like to think that anything bad might have happened to her – or, at least, nothing worse than happens to the rest of us.

I still remember the bright blue of the Aegean, the garish reds and greens of Anthony's canvases, the rakish angle of the policemen's caps as they stood on the beach with their arms folded, watching my departure. As the last ferry slid away from the shore, I sat with my back to my future. Anna nursed quietly as I kept looking at what had once been my home. I swayed in time to the rhythm of the waves, patted her as Mama had once patted my arm.

In the fading light of evening, the sand gleamed like bone.

Judith Mok

Pirates

'My name is Rashid Gallili.' He hears his voice echoing loudly against the houses and the wet asphalt.

Not loud enough. She is still cupping her ear with her hand, her slightly open mouth very close to his cheek.

'Could you greet the King for me?' she whispers. Pink lipstick stuck in the cracks around her lips.

She wants to know how the King is. It does not matter what he shouts in her ear; she's obviously deaf. She is holding her brittle frame very upright underneath a massive mink coat.

He has offered to carry her shopping home for her and she has graciously agreed, only because she immediately recognized him as an Iranian compatriot. It turns out to be a major task as she takes bird-like steps and the bags are heavy. How much could an old lady like that need, he wonders? After he's tried to tell her his name and she's inquired after the King's health, their conversation has stopped and the noise of the traffic takes over, hissing in the rain.

His daughter Lilly rang him today, an event that never fails to make him feel inadequate. She's six already and lives in the countryside with her mother.

Lilly wanted to know if they had television there too. Where? Oh, in Dublin. He laughs out loud now that he thinks about their chat. How he tends to forget that he lives in Dublin, that he met this woman there who seduced him. He was a virgin, hardly spoke any English. She took him, straight from Tehran, home to her turf fire. Came to see him five months later with a pregnant tummy. Just to show him what happens when you sleep with a woman. Left again, disappeared. Months later he tracked her down, she and the baby, and gave her all his savings. She took the money and slammed the door in his face. He did not even know the baby's name. But he did tell his mother in Tehran on the phone that she had a granddaughter.

Lilly had been moved around by her mother a lot, finally to the countryside. It was always difficult to find them but he had to be sure the child ate well and was properly looked after. The mother never talked to him, just took money and food from him. As she had taken him in one night when she was ovulating and ready to conceive with a total stranger.

She wanted a baby, that's all. His Lilly.

He still lived in Dublin and now Lilly was talking to him on the phone about a pirate movie she'd seen. The pirates had abducted a little girl and wanted big gold coins in return for the girl. Beautiful shiny yellow coins with the head of a crowned king on them. Her voice modulated into an even higher pitch of excitement as she told him the apotheosis of the story: how they found lots of coins and the girl was saved. Did they have coins like that in Dublin? Could he send her some? When were they going to watch a movie together? Bye, Daddy. Abruptly she hung up, before he could answer any of her urgent questions.

They stop in front of a Georgian building. He waits patiently as the old lady fumbles with her keys, opens the door and turns around to thank him with her back to the steep stairs. He offers to carry the bags upstairs for her. And again she agrees. What is it she has in these bags? He keeps wondering at their weight.

Her apartment is very big and bare. The walls are painted in uneven shades of white, the curtains are heavy with dirt and there seems to be only one functioning light bulb. The grandiose-looking crystal lamps all reflect the opaque darkness around them. On the floor beside the fireplace there are magnificent porcelain bowls and Persian silver platters.

She gestures towards the bags in a casually imperious manner, could he place them beside the platters? With her crooked hands she places oranges, lemons, pineapples on the bowls and platters. Arranges the fragile leaves of the clementines around the platter. I am Mrs Bahreini she says and comes towards him to shake hands. Would he care for some coffee?

He follows her into the vast kitchen. Crusty paint on the walls, grim light, the only warmth comes from the flicker of the gas flame. She hands him his coffee in a weightless cup. Persian porcelain. Wedding gifts, her husband died ten years ago, no children in case he would like to know. Would he like to drink his coffee in the library?

She lights candles because none of the lamps seem to be working. A thousand and one books on the shelves for him to look at, and perhaps later, he might read one?

Suddenly he has an idea: why not let him fix up her apartment in return for his reading some books in her library. Or maybe she has enough friends who could fix up her place? Friends? A helpless movement from her crooked hands. A dry cackle, her Irish friends are scarce, dear. She feels her way around in the dark for a book that she must show him. When she has found the book she reads it out to him in her elegant old-fashioned Persian.

There seems to be a bird so small in Persia that it can fly through a large keyhole. It is called an *iris susah*. Look how wonderful this feathered gem is! In the candlelight her face is different, lit up by dreams. Or wishes. Does he know what *iris* stands for? It's just a misspelling of Irish. That is her firm belief. She laughs at her own joke. There must be a bird similar to the *susah* in Ireland. That is why they moved here in the first place, to look for rare birds.

She was so sad when her husband died. She is still sad. Rashid can come back and paint the place. Read all he likes. It is late. He bows over her bony hand. It feels like an accolade to death.

Goodnight, Mrs Bahreini.

He walks home through the dark, thinks of what he neglected to tell her. That the King is dead. Even the Shah is dead. The Ayatollahs are alive. That's why he is going to his Dublin home, that's why he is getting this soaked.

Good Morning, Mrs Bahreini.

He has time enough to repair her appliances, buy paint, work away at her sad walls and tell her cleaning lady to wash the curtains. Mrs Bahreini, dressed in her furs, all set to go out, listens to his stories about his pupils at Trinity College, where he teaches Persian Studies for a couple of hours a week. She is standing in the hallway waiting for him to get changed into his work clothes. There are Persian sweets on the kitchen table, and bread, coffee, and plenty of fruit of course. Is he allowed to eat what reminds her of home, her decorative display in the bowls on the floor? He is. She will get more now that she knows somebody who can carry her bags.

Then off she goes in hat and gloves, bird watching in the Irish wetlands.

He likes the manual labour; it reminds him of his first year in Dublin when he was working on the scaffolds. He earned enough to be able to study. English. He was twenty and a virgin.

Because his mother had warned him not to use it with women, certainly not without protection. It had made him anxious about the act. But when he arrived here there was so little light that all aspects of life seemed to have lost their contour. Even that woman Mary did not seem like a real woman, like in Persia. She didn't smell of flowers or move with grace. She was plump and warm and she said they could do it, she was a nurse, she was safe. So he used it and it felt comforting to be with her. Even for the one night.

The night Lilly was conceived. He paints frantically now, thinking of the hospital where Mary used to work. How he went looking for her when she had left him, yet again, without any information as to their whereabouts. The hospital wouldn't give him her telephone number. He sat there for hours, thinking hard. He told a doctor, who knew Mary and Lilly, that he was Lilly's father and that he had cancer and wanted to see Lilly for the last time. He got her phone number. All he wanted was to make sure his daughter was safe. He had no interest in her, Mary, he kept telling her. She finally allowed him to recognize Lilly officially at the registry office. She allowed him to give them money and she allowed him to see Lilly once a month.

In the village where they now lived, Lilly would take him around to the butcher's and the baker's to show him off: her daddy from Iran. Persia, he tells her again and again. They talk on the phone once a week.

He spends ten days doing up Mrs Bahreini's place. The crystal chandeliers sparkle. When she comes home from her expeditions he lights a fire. They read, talk or sit in silence staring at the abundance of fruit on the platters until the memories of their homeland come to them. They sometimes sing a song and cry.

No money changes hands between them. She insists on presenting him with a few good bottles. He accepts and that's that, nothing else. He enjoys being there. Thank you, Rashid. Thank you, Mrs Bahreini.

A long week later, he finds it is Sunday again. He takes his walk along Sandymount Strand, breathes the sea air, marvels at the variety of light, the lack of blue. He comes from a blue country himself. He has lunch at an Iranian restaurant, chats with random diners and waiters.

Late in the afternoon he goes home. In the entrance hall of his apartment he automatically checks his letterbox. The caretaker has left a package on top of it. A heavy envelope. On Sunday. He doesn't even take off his coat, as soon as he is in his flat he rips the envelope open. A letter from Mrs Bahreini. A present from her. She writes to him about the bird. She is getting tired of looking for it, nothing compares to the *susah*. There is a bird here in Ireland called the goldcrest, alright, it is small and could probably squeeze itself through the key hole of, say, an old convent door, God forbid. Yet it is lumpy in comparison to her favoured one. The Iris is probably lost to Celtic civilization. It was the name that made her think of it: Gold Crest. She still had some old gold coins from the King's era. Remember them? With His Majesty's head on them. She's decided to give him a couple, as a thank you for all the work he has done for her.

They spill out on the floor, large yellow coins, five of them. They look like remnants from Ali Baba's treasure. Lilly. She would love to have them.

He takes three of them, wraps them individually, carefully, and then puts them together in a little box with her name and address on it. The next morning he rushes to the post office, registered and express, please. The woman behind the counter stares at him with contempt. Who could get this worked up on a Monday morning? Silly man. Where is he from at all? Persia. She nods in broad understanding. That explains it.

He rings Mrs Bahreini to thank her for the coins. No answer. Somehow it hurts him a little to imagine the phone ringing in that lonely space.

He teaches them about his country. Pale students, already tired of a life that hasn't yet started. Exhausted by the idea of having to record all that information in their hung-over brains. He looks discreetly at bulging belly buttons, the white, tender flesh spilling over tight trousers. Citrus trees, mimosa, clean tiled walls, splendid colours are what he wants now.

Back home the phone rings. Lilly. She sounds so happy. She just got the coins. Did he get them off the pirates? Is he a pirate himself now? He answers yes to every question. Now that I have the coins can I stop being a little girl, Daddy, can I be a pirate too, Daddy? Can I?

Yes. Yes, you can.

Christine Dwyer Hickey

Esther's House

Since turning onto the quays I had been growing more and more anxious as the buildings and bridges continued to become more familiar. By the time we reached Ormond Quay Lower I was whining. Why could we not at least visit Mother, I demanded to know. Why? Why? Why?

My aunt offered me the usual excuse of Louisa's mumps.

I knew nothing about mumps except that boys my age were advised to steer well clear of them and that they were responsible for this compulsory six weeks' stay of absence, which I was now only half-way through. In any case I thought it a bit much that I should be punished for my sister's carelessness and all because I happened to be a boy.

'Poor Louisa,' my aunt said, 'hardly able to budge off the sofa, face up like a big balloon, God help her.'

But I saw nothing unusual in this, Louisa spent most of her time lolling on the sofa and she was a hefty lump besides, taking after my father for her jowly jaw. As far as I was concerned she had always had the mumps and so any sympathy I had I was keeping for myself.

The tram paused mid-quays taunting me with a view of Capel Street and I rushed across the aisle, kneeling up on a seat there and pressing my hands to the window. I could see the breast of my father's pub and that the cellar grid was up. I imagined Farley down in the dark there, like the mole in the hole that he was, muttering away to himself as he went about his work, only lifting his face to the light whenever a swish of dress hem passed overhead.

I looked up to the sign above the front door – *Select Accommodation for Artistic Performers. Music Rooms Available. Best Weekly Rates* – so clear I could trace the letters with my finger through the glass of the tram. Soft blisters of white lace from the open windows on the floors above the pub and in the next-door building – my mother's guesthouse taking its morning airing. Even my own bedroom window in the attic was up, and I felt the intrusion. Nobody ever bothered with my room, except for myself, and I wasn't there. I was here with Aunt Esther.

I tried to guess which window Mother was behind and what she might be doing there. Or Carolina – where would she be? Down in the back kitchen riddling the cinders. Out in the yard squeezing the guts out of newly washed linen. Up in one of the music rooms maybe, frantically hawing a shine out of a piano?

But before I could settle on a definite picture of Carolina, the tram gong sounded and the view rattled out of my sight.

My aunt's voice came out behind me, in that slightly bewildered tone she kept for onlookers and impending scenes. 'Your mother is up to her eyes. Now be a big boy for goodness sake. Nursing Louisa, poor, poor Louisa. Between that and the Italians! I don't know how she ... well. Surely you *must* understand?'

'What Italians?' I asked spinning around.

'The opera company dear – you know?'

'Nobody said anything to me about any opera company.'

'They're staying with your mother for the season. I told you that already.'

'No you didn't tell me,'

'Excuse me, I did so.'

'No you did NOT.'

My aunt leaned her face into mine, our two mouths so close then that I had to clamp my lips together to stop from swallowing her words; there would be tea later if I behaved myself, a trinket from Pimms, lemon sherbet from Nobbits then – what do you say?

But these promises, issued as they were, through clenched teeth, sounded more like threats than treats. I shrugged my arm free from her kid-gloved grip.

'Oh suit yourself then,' she snapped.

'I wish I could get away from you,' I snarled up at her.

'And I away from *you*.'

After three weeks together we had long outpassed our initial phase of politeness, being far too intimate for that.

Every evening after supper my uncle would start the interrogation. I came to know his form; tongue dragging a last lick along the flat of his knife, hand pushing the plate away then returning to the back of the chair where it jangled the buttons on his park ranger's jacket until his tobacco pouch had been located.

'Well then,' he would begin, swiping his supper-greased fingers through coarse ginger hair, 'so tell us now what did you get up to today?'

I never minded his questions, even the ones that he produced second time round, slyly reshaped to trip me up. Indeed had it not been for my Aunt's jittering over the crockery and cutlery I might have looked on this time of the day as a welcome opportunity to engage in conversation. There was little else in the way of company for me here; my aunt or the cats were the size of it. And I hated the cats, their foolish names and pissy smell, the way they were always on the make for a scrap of food or the warmth of a recently vacated bed, an armchair, or a coat left on the sofa. Their mechanical purring and deranged night time crying, the presumptuous way they rubbed themselves off your leg – I hated their very nature.

Whatever it was that my uncle was after with his questions was still, at this stage, unclear to me, although it was obvious that Chapelizod bridge or rather something on the far side of it, had some significance, for all questions seemed to come to the bridge: had I seen it, had we crossed over it, did I notice the shop on the other side, what about that skinny oul one in the bockity house on the way up to the next village hanging over the half-door like a horse all day?

I had often heard it said by Carolina that my aunt's 'little peculiarities' were down to the bad match she had made.

'She could have had anyone,' according to Carolina, 'Anyone! with her face and figure and that voice like an angel. Pity she didn't take a leaf out of your mother's much more sensible book.'

But I saw little difference between the two husbands. Except for my uncle's colouring and bramble of a beard they were even similar in appearance. Both were quiet men, not easily lured into conversation – although my father could manage pub banter well enough, or at least roll out the same few sentences all day long for the benefit of each new customer. Both men ate with their faces close to the plate and thought nothing of belching or scratching in public.

If anything, I found my uncle to be the gentler of the two; his presence much less demanding.

And at least he would talk to me, but only when my aunt

wasn't pinned to my side. This would have to be first thing in the morning while it was still nearly dark and he was fumbling around making his lunch or eating his breakfast. I might come across him out in the garden, sitting on a log in fine weather, the outhouse when it was raining, eating his sandwiches as if he was miles away from his own kitchen table. A few times he took me with him on his rounds. Then he would nearly always ask me about my father's business:

'So how is your oul fella doing these days? – raking it in I don't doubt.

How many has he working for him now? – a right houseful I suppose.

Does the pub be busy? Packed to the gills, I suppose.

Would you say he did well for himself? He certainly did, all considered.'

As he tended to ask questions he answered himself, there wasn't too much for me to do on these chats, but for all that I wasn't ungrateful.

* * *

Every time I left my aunt's house the light always came as a shock; the amount of sky. I was used to a dark house, for we lived on one of the darkest streets in the city. But the darkness in my aunt's house was different. On the hump of a hill at the side of the Fifteen Acres in the Phoenix Park, surrounded by an inner circle of dark green railings and an outer circle of trees, the house itself was angular enough in shape – except for the ill-named sun room which bellied out onto the garden – yet it gave the impression of being completely round. No shortage of windows either but somehow the light always skulked outside.

That day my Aunt was even more agitated than usual. She even forgot to feed the cats, and I didn't remind her. Keeping a hard hold of my hand all the way down the hill from the house, never letting go, even as she shoved us clumsily through the turnstile gate into Park Lane. Her step didn't slow up until we came to the village, and I could feel the effort this cost her.

'We're just going as far as the bridge to give this little chap a look at the swans, as far as the bridge I told to him, but no further, for he'll give me no peace till he sees the swans.'

This was the announcement she made to anyone we happened to pass: the greengrocer up on a footstool struggling with his awning; the group of women waiting on the midday tram into town; the nurse pushing a baby carriage from one of the grander houses that led up to Knockmaroon Hill and the Strawberry Beds; all had to hear about the swans – not that anyone appeared too interested. It was almost as if she was asking their permission.

I had never really noticed anything odd in my aunt's behaviour, until I came to stay with her, apart from the fact that when she came on a visit to our house she couldn't seem to stop talking. My mother said this was because she was lonely and that it wouldn't kill us to indulge her a little with the occasional nod or smile. Which we did, often for what seemed like hours on end, my aunt chattering away about little or nothing, while the tea grew cold in the pot and skin grew over the jam. In her own house she rarely spoke. She spent a lot of time looking in the mirror too, not the way my mother would do with some sense of purpose, to fix her hair or rouge up her cheeks and sigh discontentedly at some aspect of her appearance. Aunt Esther just stared blankly in. And she was always so gentle, in movements as well as in voice. Yet she played the piano with something like violence. If a knock came to the door she wouldn't answer it, but came looking for me to do so, even if I was out in the garden or already asleep in bed. And now there was this business of lying to strangers about my wanting to see the swans.

We got to the bridge and my aunt tugged me over it, so sharply that I saw nothing of the swans and little of the river other than a vague shimmer of glittering worms to the corner of my eye.

'But what about the swans?'

'On the way back.'

It was a long trek, all uphill after that, and far too warm for October. Pinned by the sun to a high stone wall that seemed to have no intention of ending, I struggled behind my aunt, heels dragging behind me, sweaty body wriggling against my wool suit, head boiling under my cap. I sent up the occasional sigh of distress, each one of which was duly ignored.

At last a stretch of railing broke into the wall, then a gate flanked by two tall round pillars. Here we stopped. And still she said nothing.

I looked up at the sign arched over the gate: *Stewarts Hospital for Imbecile Children.*

I recognised the word 'Imbecile', having heard my father use it often enough to his unfortunate counterhands and was curious to see how this might apply to children. My aunt pushed me towards the gate.

She tucked herself in behind a pillar, her back to the railings, a handkerchief muffling her mouth as if she'd been appalled by a sudden smell. I could barely hear her instructions.

'What do you see?'

'Nothing really, just trees, a bench, a big building, a veranda.'

'Step closer. Now. Can you see any people?'

'A sick-nurse. No two. Two nurses.'

'Nobody else?'

'Well ... yes.'

'Who? Who?'

'Sick people ... I suppose.'

'Is he there?'

'Is who there?'

'Red hair. He'll have red hair. Well? Answer me – won't you answer me? Is he? Is he there?'

'I don't know. How old is he?'

'Fifteen. Can you see him?'

'Yes.'

We caught the tram home and she never opened her mouth, passing me the fare to pass on to the conductor. As the tram crossed back over the Chapelizod bridge I looked out the window, but saw no swans on the river.

As soon as we pushed through the turnstile gate back into the Park she started to sob. When we got into the house she was still at it, standing in the centre of the sun room.

'Oh my dear,' she said, 'we are in a stew. If your uncle ever finds out – such a stew.'

I looked about me at her roundy house, and the lumpy dark furniture, and the queer brown light that filled up the sun room and the two of us standing there like big chunks of meat, and I had to turn away from her then to bite the grin from my lips.

A few minutes later she called out from her bedroom for a glass of water and a green tincture bottle that I would find under the spools in her sewing casket.

I held the glass while she sipped. She was still crying although the sobs were somewhat smoother now. After a while they stopped altogether. Then she pulled back the eiderdown and asked me to get in beside her. I started to fidget, mumbling away about lessons, the amount of school I was missing, the promises I had made to Mother to keep up my singing exercises. But my aunt was having none of it. 'I'm so cold,' she said, 'so very cold.'

Then I came up with the excuse of feeding the cats.

'Just a few little minutes,' she pleaded, her voice slow and sleepy, 'that's all I ask.'

I took my time in unlacing my boots, and longer still to take off my stockings. But when I had finished her eyes were still open.

I lay with my back to her, trapped by her arms and her smells – which up to now had only come in loose passing hints – were wrapped like swaddling around me: rosewater and dress-sweat, an alkaline odour which I took to be from her medicine, a sour dry aroma that reminded me of a bonfire after all the heat had gone out of it.

My body stiff as a plank, hers soft and full as pillows behind me. Whispers tipped off the back of my neck and nestled like nits in my hair; senseless whispers about secrets, and stews, and not ever telling. Toby she said the boy's name was, fifteen last May, same age as Louisa, give or take a day.

I closed my eyes and thought of the ginger boy, the lies I had told her about him. He's reading a book, I had said, now smiling at the nurse, now talking to a boy at his side.

When I woke up there was only the sound of her sleeping breath, the faint creaking of loosened corsetry behind me.

I slid out of bed, then took my boots out to the sun room. But the sun room was still too close to her room and no corner of the house seemed to offer me sufficient distance. I put on my boots, walked through the garden and stood at the side of the Acres.

There was a whiff of distant music from the viceregal lodge and scribbles of light through the trees. And such an amount of sky!

A big black back made of sky, and the stars standing out against it were like a rash of silver scabs.

* * *

I have painted a picture for Mother. Have taken my time with it, stroke by soft stroke, patiently waiting for each colour to dry before carefully adding the next. My uncle set up the easel and brought me the paints. Sometimes he stood next to me, telling me what to do. His hand might make to take the brush off me, but in the end he always let me do it myself. He showed me how to apply colour. How to blot it off again when I made a mistake.

The picture shows my Aunt Esther's house and all the trees that surround it; dark curly evergreens and the spindly brown bones of those in full moult. The Dublin Mountains are mauve in the background, the dip of Chapelizod village; yellow and red, its rooftops peep over the Payne's grey wall of the Phoenix Park.

The deer I have relocated from the far side of the Acres where they sleep in their little scoops under the trees. Now they are sleeping on the hill beside the house. It's a bit of a cheat, but my uncle says it's all right to cheat for the sake of the picture. He says he doubts the deer would mind. My uncle knows the deer so well, when he strolls through the middle of the herd they don't scatter, just lift their sturdy necks to watch him pass by with black steady eyes. When I've finished the picture I make my signature in the corner so as Mother will always know who it came from. My uncle puts a frame around it, then wraps it in four sheets of crisp brown paper. I call my picture Esther's House.

It helps me to put in the days of the last two weeks of my stay.

In the evenings I sit by my aunt while she bashes the piano. This is after we have visited the swans and are up out of bed. I used to turn the pages for her, but I stopped doing that ages ago. She never looks at the music anyway.

While she plays I am walking myself in my mind through our house in Capel Street. I can see Mother and Carolina then, what they're like at this hour of the day when it's time to put the lights up and when they're always together. I follow them both as they move through the house, room-by-room, corner-by-corner, flight-by-flight of all our stairs. Everywhere they go they leave light behind them.

* * *

When I get home only Farley is there. He tells me Mother has gone out and that I've only just missed her.

'Gone to the train station to see off them bloody Eyeties, doubt she'll be back for a while yet. A swank tea they were having before setting out. In the Shelbourne, or maybe she said some place else?'

Then he tells me Father is with his bookkeeper and he's not to be disturbed. But there's no need for him to tell me this, as I have no intention of disturbing my father, and hadn't asked for him in the first place.

'Your sister is up in the sitting room.'

'Where's Carolina?'

'Day off.'

I go up to Mother's bedroom thinking I'll leave the picture there for a surprise, maybe hide myself behind the curtain until she finds it, pick the right moment before popping out. This plan makes me so giddy I nearly trip up the stairs.

But there's no room for the picture in Mother's room. The bed is bumpy and bright with laid-out clothes she has been trying on. Her dressing table, packed with little bottles and boxes. The mantel over the fireplace crowded with cards and ornaments. Hatboxes all over the floor. I try leaning the picture against the wardrobe door but it slides down off the mahogany surface.

There's a funny smell in the bedroom. Not just the vaguely farty smell of my father but a new sweet smell that I don't recognise, oranges and perfume maybe. There are things in the room I've never seen either, vases stuffed up with flowers and a neat fat bunch of Parma violets lying on the chair. A box of figs is open on the floor. Sorrento figs, so the lid says. There's a photograph poked into the corner of the dressing mirror; a profile I've never met, a deep black signature scrawled over one shoulder.

In the end I just leave the picture on the floor, then go to the window pulling the curtains around me.

The windowpane holds a glaze of my face, dark and devilish. It shows years I haven't yet lived, scars I haven't yet earned. It shows every minute of every day of the last six week of my life.

A ginger-haired boy and sneery-eyed cats; the shape of my aunt's bed, my boots on the floor; my uncle drifting through herds of deer. These are the images that fill up my reflection, edging in and out, swelling and shrinking, then melting slowly into my face and my chest.

I stay where I am, waiting for Mother.

VONA GROARKE

Cubs

Four fox cubs had been hung from the gate with green twine. She stopped the car. She couldn't touch them, but they were definitely dead. Their heads were faced away from the road in the direction of her house, in line with each other and all the one size. Four small bodies set by a farmer's hand into this one, choreographed death scene. Newborn. Their colour was sharper than the few remaining leaves on the two beech trees. Killed the same day. Today. While she'd been at work.

Margaret had been watching the mother for the past few weeks. As her body got bigger and her steps less prompt, she had ventured closer to the back of the house, and Margaret got used to keeping an eye out for a dash of auburn along the ditch that slumped to the back of the house. She'd wondered if she should put milk out, but what would happen then when the cubs were born and suddenly there'd be a whole litter of them prowling at her door? No, better left alone.

It must have been raining. There were still some drops on the fur of each of them. Had he killed them before he strung them up with that sickly, green twine? They were too composed for struggle and they had the look of animals that had not known to refuse anything in their foreshortened lives.

Their tails hung like pointless exclamation marks. Margaret's hand was extended towards the tip of one. She was thinking how silky they were, and what the colour reminded her of, when she noticed the flattened grass in front of her foot. A larger imprint than her own and lined across, the way the soles of Wellingtons are. He had stood here, so. Probably had thrown the bodies on the ground just to her left before dipping down to choose another to sling into the twine. Did the sight of them, or the feel of them – still warm? – relieve his sense of all the harm they'd manage, left to live? Did he have them in a sack, or had he carried them in his own arms? Did his jacket smell, even now, of their small death? Would the mother pick it up in his wake and follow him to this, her cubs arrayed with such a clean hand on the gate?

Her mother had a stole one time with a small fox-head at one end. For Christmas and funerals, and that one time they'd gone to a dinner dance. Margaret had brushed her mother's hair for her, and had helped set the fox stole down on the silver dress with the satin pink ribbon. Beautiful. Except for the black, dreadful eyes that seemed to follow hers around the room. They were, she remembered, the colour of the clutch bag her mother had bought especially, that was still in the wardrobe of the back bedroom, that she had meant a few times to throw out. She used to keep such things for her own daughter. But now she had no daughter, and no son either, and the bag was fusty and no longer smelled of perfume and compliments. Only the small fox eyes would be unchanged, wherever they were, overwhelmed by darkness, watchful as ever for that one rupture of light.

Such small heads. One would fit, almost exactly, in her palm, snout to the tip of her fingers, ears back where the thumb would cock a warning to the air. *Run. There's so little time. And I can't help you now.*

No blood on the bodies, however he'd managed it. Would she know at once, or would she think, coming over the field, that they were waiting for her? No.

'We can't leave them there. It's wrong.'

Margaret found she wasn't that surprised.

'I know.'

The voice was right behind her, maybe one step to the left. Margaret didn't turn.

'Why?'

'They say they spread disease, and they can kill if they have to, too.'

'But why here, like this?'

'I'm not sure. I haven't seen it done like this before.'

This isn't mine. I didn't do it. Don't ask me to explain.

But she did know. The sight of them deserved, at least, the words. She turned.

'To keep the mother away. She won't come here after this.'

Sarah. Her name was Sarah. No surname offered, none required. Margaret knew who she was. Or bits of it, gathered up like a paper trail, clues that had established her since the day she had arrived.

She'd had one suitcase, the same colour as her coat. It was not the kind of coat you saw often in Classen, its odd squares stitched together with comic book excess. The suitcase too was oversized, and Margaret noticed from her front window that the woman opposite had set it down with some relief. Her body had stooped in the direction of the case for a few seconds after its release, before straightening like a metronome needle fingered into place.

She'd been very still in front of a door that, even from across the road, Margaret knew was flaked with dull neglect. It had been many winters since that door had opened on anything but obsolete air and four hunched rooms that had nothing, not even furniture, to speak of.

From the look of the coat and the hair tied back in a lumpy ponytail, Margaret had figured she was young, much younger than herself. She stood then like a study in shades of brown by an artist with a taste for the picturesque. She stood as though the door would open at any second to admit her to the life she had once wished for, but had never bothered to expect.

Margaret remembered how she had closed her eyes, thinking that when she opened them, there would be no woman at the house across the road. No suitcase, no house. The same artist would have decided instead on a natural scene, all grey and flitting shades of brown, unmoved by human life. That would be easier, Margaret had thought. Then I could get off to work.

But she was not gone. Her arm, without a trace of briskness to it, was in the act of picking from the front left pocket of the copious coat, something that was probably a key. She's tired, Margaret thought. She has come a journey and the end of it is damp and dank and has no welcome for her.

And she will not stay.

The house across the road had been withering for years. Perhaps as a rebuke to its decline, Margaret's house contained itself in clean lines and definite ambitions. The front door was a smart, bright yellow and she had the gutters cleared out every spring. The garden read like a poem for children, with nothing wayward or surprising there.

From the road, Margaret's life seemed ruthlessly organised. In fact, it was not, but nothing about the polished door lock and moss-free roof would have given that away. This was a strategy; Margaret believed in a smooth exterior. She had made a life out of thinking herself tasteful, relevant and discreet. If pushed by the right person, she might have admitted that you could get away with a lot more if you didn't present to the world at large (or at least the world at Classen), a catalogue of pressure points and bruises.

Which was partly why the house opposite presented her with a personal insult. This was what happened when your life had snags in it, small clumps of darkness that were on show to anyone who cared to shift their view. The house was the result, the inevitable result, of throwing open your life, and if Margaret was sure of anything, it was that exposure of this kind meant very little but mould where it shouldn't be and breathless air that wasn't going anywhere.

Far better to make a life that had only the most obvious chinks in it: childlessness, a dead-end job, dyed hair that should have been those two tones darker. Nothing with implicit drama, just the commonplace lacks that were so general as to never need to be observed or remarked on.

That way, you never had to find yourself on the step of a house that should probably be knocked, that had loose slates and windows that wouldn't prise open, that had sycamore shoots pressing out under the walls, that nobody had thought of once since the trailer had pulled away with a bedstead, a green couch and two mattresses about four years ago. That hardly had an owner any more, unless it was the woman whose hand was even now moving upwards towards the lock.

Perhaps she had bought the place and had arrived to shake it out and breathe into its absences, a life.

Perhaps she was thinking better of it now. Certainly, she was in no great hurry to take possession of the place. If she had picked up her suitcase, turned tail and gone back towards Athlone, Margaret would have put her down as smart enough to give mistakes their due.

But she'd gone nowhere. She hadn't exactly slotted her life into the business of the place, but she was here, and it didn't look as though she planned to leave.

From that first day to now, not a word had passed between them. This was the first time Margaret had heard her voice. She guessed money from the accent. Dublin, the best schools. A way of letting the words seep into each other, like they weren't hers, like she couldn't be held accountable for whatever they might change.

She was standing now between Margaret and the cubs. Faced towards them. Even saying the words, Margaret realised, had made her seem complicit. One of *them*. She spoke anyway.

'I'll untie this side. You do over there.'

'What will we do with them?'

Indeed.

'Will we put them in the ditch?' Even saying it, Margaret knew she sounded pinched, ungenerous.

'They have to be buried.'

Of course. Her voice was very sure of what it said now Margaret had nothing to match it with. Bury them. A shallow pit, the bodies in their hands, soil on their fur. At least she was not alone.

'But where? He owns both the fields, he'd never let us bury them in there.'

'In your garden?'

Oh god, no. Not that. Their four heads underneath her soil. Every colour a shade of their heads, a way of knowing how death would still their efforts and their claims.

'Could you not ...?'

'It's not mine. I promised I wouldn't change anything.'

'Say nothing, so. The weeds will keep your word for you.'

When she came back with the spade and shovel from the

garden shed, Sarah had taken off her coat and set it on the grass. The bodies were muffled in the deep brown of the winter coat.

'Will it not be ruined?'

What?

'It doesn't matter. I can brush it off.'

She can brush off death. She can show up behind me and talk like we were always friends. She can put her life down in that cottage, between damp walls and fetid air. She can do anything. She can show me how.

'Will I take this end?'

'Yes.'

So polite, between them. No loose ends.

'Now?'

'Now.'

There was no weight in them. The furthest corner from Sarah's cottage was a small clump of vetch and weeds. They dug behind it, a thin hollow that didn't seem to grow deeper no matter how thickly they dug. The last of the light was stacked up in the west behind Sarah's head. Margaret noticed a line of sweat beading the other woman's upper lip. She was too hot herself, but Sarah had no coat on, only a light shirt, (a man's shirt?), and some jeans. Her hair was filthy, and even in this cold, Margaret could smell acrid sweat every time the other woman shovelled out a cusp of earth and dropped it on the neat heap by the wall. Of course, there probably was no shower in the house. Or hot water, either, unless she boiled it up.

'You won't see it from the house. It'll be behind the weeds.'

'I'll remember it.'

Matter of fact. The voice parched of feeling and any depth.

'Will that do?' She knew they should go deeper, but she hadn't the stomach for any more of this. They were only small. What they'd done would do.

'The rest is rocks.'

Was she crying? The way she said 'rocks' had a hill in the middle of it, and two sides, both of which were in full darkness now. Margaret couldn't see her face, the way she turned away a little towards the cottage. She should have asked her to go in and put on the light. But she was not in charge here. This was not her house, and those were not her half-breaths that could have been sobs, or were maybe just a sign of exertion when you were only used to sitting in a house in darkness, doing god knows what.

'We'll lift the coat over and tip them in.'

Margaret's earlier impulse to touch the bodies was gone. They'd be so cold.

Sarah said nothing, but lifted the cubs off her coat and laid them, one by one, in the shallow pit. She lay them as they had hung, close together and facing to the right. Kids in a sleeping bag, Margaret was thinking. When the messing is finished and tiredness has kicked in.

Sarah had started on the infill: rhythmical, close strokes that spread darkness over them. Darkness that was hardly different now from the dark of the road, or what was splayed in the branches of the ditch. Sarah too had been claimed by its edgy grip. Margaret felt the whole world around her was slipping away, and only she could see where it all would fall.

The heap they had made at the side had levelled out. Margaret had done hardly anything but watch. She patted the mound with the back of her spade and Sarah looked over at her in a gesture of surprise. Margaret clutched at a few of the weeds that had seen out the frost. She lay them on the grave. They looked ridiculous, but she couldn't exactly stoop to pick them up.

So what?

What now? Ask her over for coffee? Hardly. See does she need anything?

Sarah was pulling up her coat from the ground, shaking out whatever she could loosen from its cloth. She didn't put it on herself, but folded it over her arm and, looking at it still, said, 'Thanks.'

As though Margaret had been only the helper and Sarah the one who had really suffered. Margaret, perennial handmaiden. Living alone in a house she never earned.

She went back to move her car. The frozen stuff in the boot would be thawed by now, the pizza base soggy and the peas shrivelled up. Too late for coffee anyway, or she'd never get to sleep. She sat in the car without quite turning the key.

There were no lights in the cottage either, and the whole road and both the gardens were consigned to darkness now.

Rebecca O'Connor

St John of the Miraculous Lake

For fear of the sound of his own voice. This smooth-skinned, nettle-eyed child won't open his mouth for fear of the sound. He goes up to the old hospital and throws seven boy's names, six girl's names, five fruit at the wall, jumping and spinning each time before catching the ball. But the words stay in his head.

Sometimes he plays nurses with the girl next door. He lies still as a doll while she jabs him with lollipop sticks until his willy stiffens in his trousers. In his head he is saying 'Yes nurse,' 'It hurts just there,' 'Thank you nurse.'

He is like St Bernadette of Lourdes. Except that he is a boy. And he hasn't seen the Virgin Mary. And he doesn't live in France. Can't even speak French. But he *is* a saint, he knows that much for sure. Heard people say he was touched, people who thought he might be deaf as well as mute. It's only one ear is deaf. The other one can hear just fine, thank you. He feels most holy when he stands at the window at dusk looking down at the lake. For it is a lake of holy water, healing water. Oh, to go there, but there is no going there anymore. Not even when the weather changes. Not even when he is grown.

That lake water never got warm. But they used to go there, he and his older brother – as often as they could, and as soon as they could – not long after you could see your own breath, and before the air was abuzz with midges. Swimming near to the jetty was the thing, where you could feel the tadpoles nibble at your skin. It was a peculiar sensation, skin burning with the cold and them nibbling. They scooped the jelly into buckets and brought it home, to watch it turn. But they always just missed that moment when the spawn became full-grown frogs – too careless, too preoccupied, or too subtle a change to see, whatever it was.

It was down there he had one of his visions, only he saw nothing. There was a moment when suddenly it got warmer, suddenly the birds were making more noise, more flutter, when the air became visible like a swarm, and he looked up at the chinks of sky between the trees as if they were blue bees. His head back until his neck cricked, his feet slowly sinking into the mulch. The insects humming, whirring. And the sound of Ben thwacking branches to either side of him with a stick. It was the sound of a small wood fire, but it wasn't. It was Ben saying 'Come on, we've got to find him,' and pushing through the undergrowth. Then the noise stopped. He stooped to flit a stone across the lake. It sputtered, made a single ripple, and sank.

He even went back and looked for Jake in the shed. As if they'd forgotten him, as if their wee brother hadn't been with them only a few minutes before. It was that kind of vision: though he saw nothing, he could feel time running him round like a headless chicken. He looked in the old tumble drier – Jake's favourite hiding place – but he wasn't there.

Of course he wasn't. He was with Ben.

But he wasn't with Ben.

He went down again to the jetty and found Ben on his hunkers looking for perfect skimming stones.

'He's about here somewhere,' he said, 'the little shite. He's hiding.'

That was the sort of thing could make you laugh, Ben talking like he was grown up. But he started to cry instead.

They hid in the shed, looking at the pictures in their children's bible, and in Ben's comics, eating cola bottles and space ships. They said nothing. Wasps flittered in and out of their paper nest on the ceiling. Then Ben went behind the upturned table with the broken leg and John into the tumble drier. Soon his legs went dead. He liked it, and he liked the smell of dust and turpentine and unwashed vegetables. But he was scared too. Then he heard his father's voice calling, and that was when he had his second vision. It was a smaller one than the first: he only got a kind of ringing in his ears, and the inside of the tumble drier went white with light for a second and then was dark again, darker than before. His father was calling 'Be-en! Jo-ohn! Ja-ake!', his voice all odd and tinny. Then the lid was off, and he was lifted free of the drier, his legs frozen and a horrible swelling pain in them that made him want to knock his knees from their sockets.

'Where's Jake?' his father was saying. 'Where's Jake, where's Jake, where's Jake,' and shaking him. Then shaking Ben.

He never spoke after that. His mother went like a baby, like Jake used to be, with swollen eyelids and blubbery lips. Her tongue grew enormous, and her skin all blotchy. His father was jaundiced-looking. They both terrified him, as did the neighbours with their freshly laundered hankies and soapy hands, lifting him off the ground, lifting him on to their unfamiliar warm laps with tears swilling in their eyes. Ben was too old for sitting on laps. He didn't want them touching him. He sat away from them – near their mother, always near her – and watched. It was after he had told them we only wanted to show Jake the frogs, only wanted to show him where they lived, take them grown up frogs back home.

And after they'd gone to look, and then found Jake in the holy water, and sent him to the hospital, the one that's closed now, and left him there for good.

Then the bottom bunk was empty. John carried on talking to his baby brother anyway, just like he always did, except in his head. Words flooded through him, drowned him.

Then his mother removed the bunk and replaced it with a single bed.

He isn't used to sleeping so close to the ground so he's started bedwetting and falling out. Now he has a dark green plastic sheet he sleeps on so when he pees himself it doesn't go down into the mattress. He hates the smell of his own pee. He hates the cold mackintosh feel of the under-sheet. It reminds him of this one time when they went up into the mountains and it rained and rained, and all they had to eat were Rich Tea biscuits. Sometimes he hears Ben crying and goes in his room and says 'Ben' and Ben says 'What?' and he says 'Nothing'.

His mother has taken to wearing a pendant around her neck with a little picture of Jake, which she kisses every night before bedtime. His mother tells him Jake is an angel up in heaven. He is the boy in the bottom bunk, underneath him; it's hard to think of him up above. But he does. And he says prayers every night and asks him to look over him, even though he's underneath. When he prays it is so quiet that he can hear moths flutter against the light in the hallway. And when he's in bed the dim light through the window over the door stings his eyes, but he won't let his mother turn it off. Then he hears her, and he closes his eyes tight, feeling her shadow move across them and the warmth of her body stooping over him. Her breath smells of cloves.

'Are you sleeping, John darling? Are you? Don't you worry, everything is going to be all right. Mammy loves you very much.

You say a wee prayer for me, hah? And for Ben, and for Jake. You're my little angel. What would I do without you? I'm awful tired ...'

The trick for getting rid of her is to moan and turn over on to his deaf ear so's he can't hear her anymore. He hates this mother who comes to him in the night.

He needs one more vision to secure his place in heaven at the right hand side of God. It's the only place will do, otherwise he'd feel like he was missing out. But the visions have all dried up lately. His front tooth is loose. That could be a sign. And the girl next door has stopped speaking to him. Maybe she senses something. They were supposed to get married, now she won't even look at him. Maybe the next miracle is to stop his mother crying all the time. Then the whole neighbourhood would raise him up on eagle's wings, make him to shi-ine like the *SUN*, he sings (in his head of course). Oh praise be to St John of the Miraculous Lake! He can hear them clear as day.

He knows what to do. And so he gets himself a bucket from the shed, a long time after Jake has been away, and he makes his way down to the lake, the forbidden place. He doesn't meet anyone he knows on the road. Safe over, and over the stile into the field that leads down to the swimming place. It is the place of the first miracle, the sacred place. He steps tentatively in, crouches down and drags the bucket through the water. One bucket of holy water is all it will take. One bucket will fill the whole basin where they used to keep the frogs. And then it will be the holy fount, and people will come to him to be healed. And he will heal his mother, and his father, and Ben. He will wash away their weirdness, Amen, Gloria in Eggshells! That's what they'll say at his first communion, when he's brought up before the priest on the altar, bathed in light.

The water is soaking through his trainers.

Next thing there's somebody in the field, a flurry of colour running towards him. He turns his back on her. Maybe she won't see him, or know it's him. He needs more time. He needs to be able to get the water back up to the basin. But when he turns to look she's still running, and it's clear now that it's his mother. He tightens his grip on the handle of his bucket. There's mud on his hands. She's nearer, scooping him up with words; then she's here taking him right up in her arms. He clings, water splashing over the sides of the bucket onto his hands.

'Put it down,' she says, grappling with his fingers.

It falls away, splashes into the water. Then he knows the only thing he can do is save her alone, so he slowly raises his eyes up to hers, lifts his muddy hand, and dabs her forehead with the holy water. He holds her, very quiet, very still, while her eyes dry into the lake.

'Put it down,' she says.

Molly McCloskey

Here, Now

Out here, where home is – 12 miles from town, 132 from the capital, latitude 54 degrees 20 minutes, longitude 8 degrees 40 – we're at the centre of our universe. Our peninsula: tiny feline tongue-flick into the endless liquid of the Atlantic. *Cape Neurotic, breakaway republic, bandit country* – all pet names, only the first of which I've ever understood. Much further north and you're AWOL, into the too-high wilds of Donegal. But here, despite the silence, we seem not too far from anywhere. Silence that sometimes – like a climber's nightmare, a hidden cleft – feels like the firm earth having suddenly given way beneath us, dropping us irretrievably into dark and hollow. Only an illusion; we're on solid ground here. Nestled between mountain and shoreline, or rise and fall, able anytime to look left, or right, and be shown what it is we're relative to.

From where we are (as from a lot of places now), the new highways radiate like spokes from the hub we imagine *here* is, drilling past the now redundant, serpentine old laneways (recall: the shock of rod and spiral, side-by-side on the small slide, your very first turn at the microscope). Suggestion of stark choice, between what demands but rewards, and the line of least resistance. Roads hastening us in three directions, towards Galway, Dublin, Donegal. Roads referred to not by name but by order of appearance: Old and New. As though there would only ever be two versions of a thing, or ever one definitive account.

SUMMER

Reneged-on promise, spring's failure to deliver, *coitus interruptus* of a season. Worse somehow than winter, which, at the very least, arrives. I haven't learned it, the fine art of pessimism. How to stop expecting. *Teach me*, she wrote, before departing, *what I have to have to live in this country.*

THE NEW ROAD

Which you and I didn't live to see. Lying in your upstairs bedroom all that dank summer of its construction, its tripartite beat tripping off our tongues. Eight-point-eight kilometres of sudden superhighway and right outside your door. The changes it would bring! As though it were the coming of the motor car itself. Here to there in no time flat; what we couldn't do with a proper passing lane. How what for eons had been villages would overnight begin to feel like 'suburbs'. We hadn't much else to talk about, which doesn't mean they weren't good nights.

Autumn, and someone else by then. Talk of the highway assumes the present tense. The local paper runs a front-page piece on how to navigate a roundabout. The Sunday drive assumes proportions it never dreamed of. A *dual carriageway*. Could the term be any more charming, or less appropriate? And each time a new one opens, we shave minutes off the trip to Dublin. As if through some polite willingness on our part to illustrate a proof of plate tectonics, we inch ever closer to the capital.

THE OLD ROAD

Despite my love of speed and the queer way that vast, industrial swath through the scree appealed to me, when coming to you I stuck instead to the old road. With its bad bends, its fog banks, its stray cows come upon round corners and our own agreement that the new way was far less arduous, the old nevertheless maintained a coy hold on my loyalty. As though to remind me of where I'd come from, or of the condition in which I'd first arrived at your door. Slow and inefficient, knotted.

The old road bearing the weight and imprint of all those winter nights I travelled to and from you. Who I was, or who you were, on any given Friday. My stabs at perpetuity. My way of saying I'll keep returning to wherever you are, somehow the same, somehow fortified against change, against age and the flux of season and the occasional fit of pique. My way of knowing that we have been here, again and again, at your huge hearth at the end of each workweek, swapping laconically the details of our lives. Who you pined for, or who I did. Long-distance liaisons. Sound advice. Constancy and repetition and yet the bloom of things too. For laconic as we were, we were not immune to wonder, imagining we saw our very souls ripen under the watchful eyes of time and mutual regard.

HERE

At dawn or on summer evenings, the landscape an inversion of itself, things assuming their complementary colours: a yellow sky; Benbulben, which I know to be green, now a deep magenta. Five hundred twenty-six metres high and always there, in its uncanny self-possession, its horizontal thrust, its air of presumption and demand. Depending on the light, the angle, my own mood: priapic jut, or extended arm ushering me in, and northward. And to the south, its other: dome to its mantel, afloat while it is all full steam ahead. Self-satisfied, too, but afterwards, and in repose. Flat on its back and pooling like an ample breast.

PARKING DISCS

To the introduction of which nothing definitive could be attributed. Not the end of an era, not the mark of our entry into the grown-up world of cineplexes, bottle banks, espresso bars and, yes, the sex shop. But something. A kind of attrition.

In the beginning, we parked in cul-de-sacs or on the outskirts. Or we cheated – 'recycled' – carefully arranging on the dash hair squeegees, ballpoint pens or cigarette lighters over the already scratched squares of our tattered parking discs. We swapped tips on hidden spaces, as though they were undiscovered holiday destinations. (That private lot smack in the centre of town, some still-virgin corner of the world.) Gradually, though, we gave in. Learned to plan ahead. Bought in bulk packets of ten, and forgot there was ever a time when we didn't have to pay to park.

The papers say we are living in a boom town, and we feel it. We feel that weird, too-quick reversal of decay. And each time something picturesque and tumbledown vanishes and something baby blue or canary yellow or forest green rises in its place, we sense the presence of allegory. Allegory is among the words we don't much use here, but we know enough to know when it's among us. Each time we forget what once existed in any given place, we are visited by a vague unease, as though we have colluded in some dubious scientific advance.

BEFORE ...

And in the company of some other you. Platonic too, but with whom so many roles were played. Who's lost, who's found, first me, then you. So that I'm waiting, uneasily, for the next reversal. Or better yet, the final incarnation of us: some sync finally fallen into, a place (on the far shore) where suspicion's banished, ethanol extinct, and gratitude so deep-ingrained it isn't necessary to refer to.

That Christmas – our cold hands calcifying round our wine glasses in the icy studio of some mutual artist friend – we clung to one another in the corner like a pair of co-dependent limpets, guffawing over my latest half-remembered scrape, and you had the backhanded good grace to say to me: *There's a good woman going to loss in there*. Two years later, some early-morning stint in your place, the heebie-jeebies now a spectator sport to me, and I'm trying hard to say the same to you – a good man – because it's true. Because I never have, and still can't.

IARNRÓD ÉIREANN

In the bathroom on the Sligo-Dublin railway line, a sign telling us how to turn on the water in the hand basin has been tampered with, so as to form a new message – the demanding, unheralded art of negative graffiti. Whole words scratched out, one 's' artfully obscured, and what we're left with is an in-joke with a world-view attached. Think of here: the affection with which ineptitude is regarded, the irony with which piety is infused. When visiting from abroad, if short on time and desiring to grasp this place in a sound bite, you might start here: *To obtain water ... pray.*

WHICH BRINGS US TO BORN-AGAIN VIRGINS

A mini-movement growing up on the far side of the Atlantic: recant your past carnality, reclaim your prelapsarian self. A sort of sexual face-lift. This news courtesy of Radio Telefís Éireann, and relayed with all the ill-suppressed mirth that such American hokum incites. Some weeks later (also via RTE, though now with quizzicality in place of mirth), this news: that the Pioneers are offering a deal. Temperance, they've decided, can start anytime. Even here, it's not about never anymore. Just two years without a drink and you too can wear the pin, be, as it were, born again. The brands of innocence we consider worth regaining. A juxtaposing that helplessly invites reduction: *the difference between us is ...* that we dream of re-imagining our sex lives; you, of alcoholic chastity.

... AFTER

That I could hand to you – *a good man*, after all – the rebirth of wonder. The chastening effect of mental clarity, emotional acuity, keenness of sensation. Strictly *bona fide* fear. In a word (so hackneyed it hurts), sobriety. No longer awash in that amniotic fluid. See it shaken from you, like excess sea water upon emerging, the evolutionary being that is you heeding an unconscious call to a next echelon. Or your own tide out, brackishness receded, detritus exposed, the dropped hints of your life – *still there* – marking the way back. Equivocal treasures you'd glean then, ugly only to the untrained eye, like the bleached skulls we see on other people's mantels, prized beyond reason for reasons other than themselves.

My Christmas list for you: an undiluted consciousness, the prickliness and nettle-itch of fresh idea, pins and needles – this time – of boyish awe, the eager jump-start of each early morning, a mind you could strike a match on. If I could see it through sufficiently, to the point where I can say I haven't failed you. To the naff soda pops and the too-much smoking. To the living gingerly, the chaperoned existence, the life as though in kid gloves. To the graceful retirement of the antihero and the point of diminishing returns. Not only reached, but recognized.

NOW

In a parking lot somewhere in New Jersey, amidst a sea of stickered bumpers (declarations of intent, pithy quips, statements of preference), one-stop wisdom shop of the New World –

There are many vacancies in the motel of the mind.
Handguns in schools: for or against?
And marvellously: *I'd rather be sailing to Byzantium.*

– there in the land of mobility and reinvention, simulation and submerged rebirthing, alien abduction and impregnation, of wishful thinking never content to remain so, one radical assertion of intransigence stands out, a lone (ironic) voice sagely, trenchantly satisfied with its lot:

I'd rather be here, now.

HOME

Always when off the train. And at just that spot. Someone said it's hard to leave here because of that configuration of mountain and shoreline, the curvature of one along the other and the way we're lodged between. Concentric vortex of an embrace, poisoned chalice, gift tax.

But always on returning from the capital it hits, the bashfulness that too much generosity inspires. Summer evenings especially, coming west by train. Three hours of hell, then ... *Carrick-on-Shannon, Boyle, Ballymote, Collooney* ... and knowing it's coming, finding it there, stepping down onto the platform, a sort of guilty glee, as though I've skipped with the booty and this is it: being here. That strangely subterranean feel to the place, to being this little bit beyond the pale and harbouring the secret of where a thing is hid.

Into the car then, down, down the hill and out of town, into the deepening quiet and the thickening dark, spelunking my way towards home. The same chagrin at my own dumb joy and just when I'm wondering what's behind it, it's there, in front of me, curving into view. That overly invoked mountain that two days ago I couldn't get shut of fast enough, over my shoulder everywhere I went, like a cheap dick on my tail, always *there*, in whatever ham disguise: pink, green, black, cut cake, 2-D cut-out, tidal wave, hung curtain, bad landscape painting, noun demanding adjectival range I haven't got. But now, seeing it afresh, I'm brought to heel, as corny as it feels. Just there. At Rathcormack, with the mountain on my right, the bay on my left, and that water-slide of a road, easing me into home. The plink of hit water. My own silent shout of delight.

... WELL AS WELL HIM AS ANOTHER ...

or so it pays to pretend. Until such time, anyway, as the clear truth of its antithesis can be admitted: that parts, while consecutive, are by no means interchangeable. That a hierarchy of affection exists – complete with petty power struggle, cut deal, bloodless coup, the tenterhook of dominion near-divested, and the pathos of the monarch unaware of plot-simmer – theocratic or despotic or with the mind-bending intricacy of the most bloated bureaucracy, but never, ever populist.

And always, long afterwards, the one we still talk about, the golden age of whatever our private civilization's been.

You? But could I ever know this before the end? Before all theory's been tested and each variable assigned value. The temptation to believe some untried proof remains.

If I'm even asking, it probably isn't you.

But your way of going on, like life was a game you'd deigned to play. Rather graciously, rather indulgently, all things considered (though granted, with an underlying gravity). Your figurative pose: winsomely awkward adult seated lotus-like in front of some board game with pretty coloured pieces and squares you can't afford to land on. Eager player, player by whatever wacky handed-down rules, consulter of box top when arbitrating chaos – kids' favourite bachelor uncle – but angling all the time to divine the grand design, the blackly comic hand of the creator (©Milton-Bradley) obvious to you at every turn. You've it sussed, you at your two levels, but to your credit aren't pretending you're not thoroughly engaged. Or that you don't know your place; fetchingly – as relatively in the dark as anyone – you aren't above availing of kid-wisdom.

Some near future, when I can take you with a grain of salt, stop concocting overblown metaphors for your existence. My fantasies now reduced to those of resignation, dead nerves, you having worn yourself thin. Once, though, it was like what I've heard of heroin: like being kissed by God. So I'm counting on the flat affect to follow. But that image won't hold up; your grip on me will loosen, after all. To the point where it's work to want you; already (sometimes), something more than simply waking is required. And after that – I hope – I'll find you there. But without the power to call up anything at all in me other than that old sardonic warmth. And I will wax eloquent for you on the matter of my latest object of desire, your by now banal presence reminding me that he – like you, like all my other little gods – will fall.

... ANOTHER

Our first touch, the coy plucking of insects off of one another's sleeves.

Oh, and you've one too. Here, let me ...

Days earlier, before we'd even spoken, I'd sat three rows behind you in a half-full theatre, imagining your hand through your hair was my own. Following your attention to where it wandered. Feeling cooler when you shed your coat. Smiling when you looked left to display, for my benefit, your profile. I thought I felt you squirm under the creaturely scent-sniff of my gaze and suddenly liked you, very much, for submitting so civilly to my inspection.

Later, when I referred to it, you surprised me by claiming that the whole mute exchange had been only in my mind. But I'm less convinced than ever. Your way of being, once I knew you, only confirming my suspicions. You were rare that way, how you could sit back and be enjoyed. Almost – I hate to say it – female, the way you gave yourself. Stealing the show like that: all object. I get it finally, the slavish love of beauty. The need to keep you in my sightline, and at my fingertips. The way, like an animal, I squirreled away sensations, stockpiling them for the cold spell to come.

LOVE AND MARRIAGE

In the kitchen of some too-long-married couple I know, I see they've retiled the walls. Over dinner, they conduct a tête-à-tête of injury and insult, the text from which they're working so highly allusive the rest of us can only hum along. We're all waiting for the split, for the relief of it. I, in fact, am betting they won't see next week. But then I think about their kitchen. The forward march of it. The things people do when we aren't around. Plugging away like that. Piling brick on brick. Surprising us with the way they keep rising from their deathbeds.

SOLIPSISM

Or a distant cousin of. Conundrum of unrequited love: that there is nothing so unlikely to arouse my sympathy or interest as your (unreciprocated) ardour for me. When what should please me more than passing hours in your company, pondering your unshakeable faith in my splendidness? Pining alongside you even, as we gaze into the near distance together, our four eyes trained on that superlative creature we've agreed is *I*. I – and I transformed by you like every other routine, workaday object when seen through your presently narcotised eyes – should be the sole subject of which I never tire.

So how is it instead that what I feel is pawed? I love you, after all, just not that way. How is it then that your own love sits between us like an intrusive third party? A crasher at our table, a morose drunk, a mourner who's so far exceeded the limits of our sympathy as to arouse resentment. Injecting into our otherwise gay little soirée the end of fun, a parental call to order, the killjoy knell of school bells, dawn. I watch, helplessly, as myself is extracted from myself. Yolk from white. Or decanted and given back to me as dregs, while you hold on to what's finest. You say I have 'taken possession' of you and yet it is I who feel owned. Where have I gone? And how can I give back to you the gift of indifference, the same indifference I once worked so hard to overcome?

Thankfully, this tells me something. That the anguish I

myself am so enjoying (over someone other than you) will never – however stubbornly it tries – create something where there is nothing. This is how I'm able to believe what beggars belief: that while I have not for one full minute failed to think of him, or performed one interior monologue but for *him* to hear, or sat still *anywhere* but that I envisioned his smiling, inexplicable entrance (never mind the fact he's out of town, out of the country, has never heard of here, and doesn't drive anyway), I – like some out-of-the-way eatery he often forgets exists – have not even occurred to him tonight.

This is how I learn the necessity of giving up, through this grown-up game of Pass the Parcel.

'RAPTURE'

Which I first heard while sitting on your porch. That screened-in affair which seemed suspended in mid-air, the way it jutted out over a mini-valley, the path cut through the trees unfurling underneath us. The constant rain, the always-saturated earth, the vertiginousness of our perch, and the delicate discordance of *Thirteen Harmonies*.

We felt straight out of *Deliverance*.

Ice melting. Or that was what you called it. Falling apart, it felt like. And then later, watching, as I failed to fall apart.

I'm thinking of a scavenger hunt, a game I used to love, and the list I'd need to help me find you: John Cage, Dusty Springfield, the Ford dealership on 202, resourcefulness, your own love of lists, that shade of blue, your spot-on send-up of the Stage Manager in *Our Town*, the library and the field beside – alive each night with lightning bugs, living by your wits, your own regained wonder (after the 'intervening years of anaesthetization'), bicycles, Bonnard, a sleek black lap-top, and 1:26 of 'Rapture'.

CHRISTMAS

Dinner and a long walk through Dromahair. Blatantly storybook, with winding lane, long spire perforating mist, duskiness congealing too quickly into night, and we seven – gloved and hatted – trudging smally through the stock-still hills. Barnacle geese in the marshy field, wintering here before their spring coupling elsewhere. And of humans? All with me in pairs, all six snug aboard the ark. Sweet platonic friendships I could frankly do without; company, under the circumstances, always worse than solitude. At home, at least, I've my familiars – undemanding silence, ritual of book and bed, arch-backed animal rising sleepily at the sound of my key turning – sticks to beat self-pity down. Self-pity, that ravenous ingrate that rises balefully at the simple act of 'bucking up' for company. Uninvited guest grossly feeding on itself. Asexual reproducer gone berserk, begetting and begetting with no apparent need for outside intervention (though the hospitality of friends will do nicely). Touch Socratic even, in its arrogance, how it runs rings round what I'm absolutely sure is reason.

But there's no reasoning with now. This time of year is cruel, and makes glaring all our lacks. You gone by then, and like a ghost beside me. You are anyone by now, though, and what's glaring is your very lack of specificity. An absence generic as a presence never could be, though on the side of each this much could be said: if present, possibility personified; if absent, failure of same.

This year's lesson: that loneliness, like a sick cell, will reinvent itself. Mutate, strengthen, grow resistant to the old remedies. That there are strains I haven't even dreamed of.

INCANTATION

Prayer at bedtime, Angelus for the secular set.

From Malin Head to Howth Head to the Irish Sea.

Swaddled in my bed, quick listen to the news, just before lights out, just checking: was there anything that happened I should know about?

From Carnsore Point to Valentia to Erris Head.

Sudden sense of smallness, shelter and inclusion. The fact that weather can be met, across the board, with only silence. Incongruous comfort of our collective ineffectuality – the few limits we do share. Why winter has always seemed the most communal of seasons. How death stymies – then binds – the living, levelling who's left as well.

From Erris Head to Belfast Lough to Hook Head.

Quiet pang of guilt. For what? For being here. Cosseted by airwaves, by four walls from the audible wind, warm, dry, safe and, really, OK. For the dumb good luck then of being here, which on the best days seems surely a remarkable omission, or oversight.

Rosslare. Roche's Point Automatic. Valentia. Belmullet ... 999 steady ... 996 and rising slowly ... Loop Head. Mizen Head. Carnsore Point. And on the Irish Sea.

Never more foreign than now. And yet, on hearing, of all things, the Sea Area Forecast, never since a child this tucked-in sensation. Crack of light under the door and life going on beyond it. Someone out there, with an eye on things. Parameters delineated. The compass-points of home. To be told where I am, and what bound by. Like the child's incantation. Universe: galaxy:

solar system: planet: hemisphere: continent: nation: state: city: street ...

... HOME

Out the back, a biopsy of *here*. Field, hill and dale. Copse, the spire at Lissadell, hunkered shrubs cordoning off holdings, red-roofed barns and one stark white bungalow. The mountain – robbed at twilight of its contours – now a prow on the horizon. Through the keyhole view I'm given – this lens eye – pan here, then here, pull back, wide angle now, see a country echo in concentric rings of just this. Or fly over it. All like a doll's house, down to diminutive detail, and knowable, you think, in one crossing. The human scale of things. The illusion therefore that you can grasp it. Learn the one thing you need to live here.

TOURISM

Moon over the back sheds on ink-blue nights. A rusty bike and wagon wheel propped against the side stone wall. The sheds, just shells of things. You see them everywhere. Candidates for conversion. But I like them roofless. The way the gable ends stand, regardless, as if holding up their end of the bargain. Every so often – out of the blue and never when I seek the thrill – it broadsides me, this scene in silhouette. I stare, like a tourist, into relative prehistory.

And you, living in the shadow of that old abbey. When I'd asked and you'd told me – *1508*, offhandedly – I was silenced. Centuries still strike me dumb, no matter what I learn, just keep seeming beyond my ken. As though I'm all jig time, quick-stop, planned obsolescence. What's coming, rather than what's gone.

Constellations, first here, now here. The stars obscured

for weeks by cloud cover and suddenly it breaks, and like the automated flick from one slide in the carousel to the next: a new view. Over and over, the strobing of the night sky. I step outside before bed and look up. Sometimes, even on the clearest nights: *nothing*: my own laziness of heart. A guilty inability to rise to the occasion. Sometimes, though, an awe that seems almost equal to the sight. A wholeness and no complaint. The *knowing*. And the not fearing not knowing.

THE HALE-BOPP

Zany name for what hung over us that summer, as though to keep us from taking miracle too seriously. Sounding to me like a dance my mother might have done forty-some years ago. Jiving at a mixer in West Philly. It used to hover, suspended dead centre above the straight stretch of the Donegal Road. And I, driving north, each time with the illusion of drawing nearer to it.

You then too. There with me and eye trained skyward, you. Not another, not yet fallen nor ever will be. But with me. Two of us then, standing, with our simple mouths agape and my heart gone out to us. In that prolonged instant of afforded joy, in which the eye-blink of wish-time was arrested. When we stood, you and I there, in a state of continuous grace, under that one always-falling star which finally, that September, fell from view.

Elaine Garvey

Hammer On

Pounding. On the move again, upstairs. Thumping across the floorboards on her fists and knees. I could defy her. I could list obscenities and shout them at her one by one. I could vandalise this house.

She said I could sleep in the room below her, as a temporary solution. I am still here. Did I travel in winter or perhaps through the night? Either way, I only recall being brought to this kitchen and the cake I was given to eat. She was watching me all the time but my bleary eyes hardly registered her. The next morning, the first morning, she tried to rouse me, rapping on the door as she walked in. I threw my shoes at the window in response, satisfied at the sound of splintering glass. You won't keep me here, I said, I shouted, I whimpered. You won't keep me here.

It's always the same day, none of this is news to me. I study the landscape, the direction of things: the river and its white foam, the road, attracting traffic, branching into crossroads and this heat, quiet and remorseless, which will turn into wet, which will turn into darkness. I do my rounds when the air is cooler, kicking at pebbles or nursing one along my instep. People pass by occasionally, nod in my direction, make their judgements. I can wait.

Sing, she says. We are rolling pastry, inching it across the table like white lava. I am not a singer. I start to hum something mindless, but this won't do. She releases her high, shivering voice, swaying her head to keep time. Songs about tea, bicycles and dear, sweet love. Upstairs, in her room, she is making a mould for me. I've seen its separate sections. For this. The line comes into my head and I whisper it to the baking dish: I belong to her.

I dream of floating in the water, an air sack drifting out towards the teeming shoals, and wake too soon. There is no peace here. She takes away my bed sheets while they're still warm with my impression, gathers all my measurements: feet to arse to tit to shoulder blades; width of neck, waist and wrist.

We won't speak of the time before, adding sugar to my tea. It's better here.

Proprietress. I upturn my teacup, slowly, smiling as she looks on. You are too kind.

Quiet frowns. Is this despair? Up to her room and the pounding begins. She might come through the ceiling one day. Hammer on, fists and tongs. Once the mould is ready for me, when I am fit for it all, when I match the edges exactly, I will leave for good. A fall into eiderdown, a gentle bounce, and then down again. This is the only way out.

Biographical Notes

CATHERINE DUNNE is the author of four acclaimed novels: *In the Beginning*, shortlisted for the Italian Booksellers' Prize; *A Name for Himself*, shortlisted for the Kerry Fiction Prize; *The Walled Garden* and *Another Kind of Life*. She has also contributed to four anthologies: *A Second Skin*, *Irish Girls about Town*, *Travelling Light* and *Moments*. Her most recent book, *An Unconsidered People*, is a work of non-fiction that explores the lives of Irish immigrants in London in the 1950s. Her fifth novel, *Something Like Love*, will be published in June 2006. She lives in Dublin.

CHRISTINE DWYER HICKEY is an award-winning novelist and short story writer. Twice winner of the Listowel Writers' Week short story competition, she was also a prize-winner in the *Observer*/Penguin short story competition. Her trilogy, *The Dancer*, *The Gambler* and *The Gatemaker*, has received wide critical acclaim, and *The Dancer* was shortlisted for the Listowel Writers' Week 'Book of the Year'. Christine has also written a screenplay for the film *No Better Man*, starring Niall Tóibín. Her fourth novel, *Tatty*, was longlisted for the Orange Prize and shortlisted for the Hughes & Hughes/*Irish Independent* Irish Novel of the Year 2005. Honorary Secretary of Irish PEN, she lives in Palmerstown in Dublin with her family.

ELAINE GARVEY is a graduate of the M.Phil. in Creative Writing at Trinity College, Dublin.

Vona Groarke was born in Co. Longford in 1964, and grew up on a farm outside Athlone. She has published three collections of poetry: *Shale* (Gallery, 1994); *Other People's Houses* (Gallery, 1999); and *Flight* (Gallery, 2002), which was awarded the Michael Hartnett Prize in 2003. A fourth, *Juniper Street*, will appear from Gallery Books and also from Wake Forest University Press in 2006. She now lives in North Carolina where she is Poet in Residence at Wake Forest University.

Anne Haverty was born in Tipperary in 1959. Her novels are *One Day as a Tiger*, awarded the Rooney Prize for Irish Literature and shortlisted for the Whitbread Prize, *The Far Side of a Kiss* and *The Free and Easy* (all published by Chatto & Windus). Her poetry collection *The Beauty of the Moon* (Chatto & Windus, 1999) was a Poetry Book Society Recommendation. She has also published a biography, *Constance Markievicz* (Rivers Oram Press/Pandora, 1988), and is one of the writers featured in *Ladies Night at Finbarr's Hotel* (Harcourt, 2000). She lives in Dublin.

Claire Keegan was born in 1968 and raised on a small farm in Wexford. She studied English Literature and Political Science in New Orleans. One of Ireland's most widely acclaimed new writers, she has won many story awards, including the 2000 Rooney Award for her debut story collection, *Antarctica*, published in 1999 in Britain by Faber & Faber and in the US by Atlantic Monthly Press.

Judy Kravis has recently published stories in *The Dublin Review* and poetry in *Metre* and the *Salzburg Poetry Review*. She has collaborated on many works with artist Peter Morgan, including *Lives Less Ordinary: Thirty-Two Irish Portraits*, *Tea with Marcel Proust* and *When the Bells Go Down: A Portrait of Cork City Fire Brigade*. Their two most recent books are *Revealing Angelica* and *The Beach Huts of Port Man'ech*. Judy Kravis teaches French literature and looks after a large garden in Co. Cork.

Molly McCloskey was born in Philadelphia in 1964. She moved to Sligo in 1989 and won the George A. Birmingham Short Story Award in 1991 and in 1994, and the RTE Francis MacManus Award in 1995. Her first story collection, *Solomon's Seal*, was published by Phoenix House in 1997, and her novella *The Beautiful Changes*, with four other stories, was published by the Lilliput Press in 2002. Her debut novel *Protection* was published by Penguin in 2005.

EITHNE MCGUINNESS is currently attending the M.Phil. in Creative Writing at the Oscar Wilde Centre, Trinity College Dublin. Plays include 'Typhoid Mary' and 'Limbo', both produced for the Dublin Fringe Festival. 'Typhoid Mary' was shortlisted for the P. J. O'Connor Awards and broadcast on RTE Radio. As an actor, Eithne played Sr Clementine in *The Magdalene Sisters* and Gracie Tracey on *Glenroe.* She has worked with many theatre companies in Ireland, including the Abbey Theatre, Passion Machine and Calypso.

JUDITH MOK was born in the artists' colony of Bergen in the Netherlands. She studied singing at the Royal Conservatory in The Hague, and at 21 became a professional soprano. She has performed worldwide and has produced numerous recordings. She has published three collections of poetry and two novels in Dutch, and writes regularly for the *Sunday Independent*. She is currently touring with her one-woman show based on the life of Molly Bloom. Her first novel in English, *Gael*, is published this year. She lives in Dublin.

REBECCA O'CONNOR was born in Wexford in 1975. Her poetry has been published in *The Guardian*, *Reactions 5* and *Poetry Review.* She was awarded the Geoffrey Dearmer prize for 'Best new poet of 2003', and was shortlisted for the New Writing Ventures Poetry Award 2005. *Poems* was published by the Wordsworth Trust in 2005, where she was a writer-in-residence. She currently lives in London.

MARY O'DONNELL is the author of three novels – *The Light-Makers, Virgin and the Boy* and *The Elysium Testament* – and a collection of short stories, *Strong Pagans and Other Stories*. She has also published four collections of poetry. She is an experienced teacher and workshop facilitator, and has taught writing in prison, schools and on the faculty of the University of Iowa's Irish Studies Program at Trinity College Dublin. She is a member of Aosdána.

JULIA O'FAOLAIN was born in London in 1932. Her works include the short story collections *We Might See Sights! and Other Stories* (Faber & Faber, 1968); *Man in the Cellar* (Faber & Faber, 1974); and *Daughters of Passion* (Penguin, 1982). Her novels include *Godded and Codded* (Faber & Faber, 1970); *Women in the Wall* (Faber & Faber, 1975); *No Country for Young Men* (Allen Lane, 1980); *The Obedient Wife* (Allen Lane, 1982); *The Irish Signorina* (Viking, 1984); and *The Judas Cloth*

(Sinclair-Stevenson, 1992). She has edited, alongside her husband Lauro Martines, *Not in God's Image: Women in History from the Greeks to the Victorians* (Temple Smith, 1973). As Julia Martines she has translated *Two Memoirs of Renaissance Florence: The Diaries of Buonaccorso Pitti and Gregorio Dati* (Little Brown, 1968). She is a member of Aosdána.

CAITRIONA O'REILLY was born in Dublin in 1973. She studied at Trinity College Dublin, where she wrote a doctoral thesis on American literature. Her poems, reviews and critical essays have appeared in many magazines. Her first collection of poetry, *The Nowhere Birds*, was published in 1999 and was awarded the Rooney Prize for Irish Literature. She currently lives in Dublin.

CHERRY SMYTH is a Northern Irish writer living in London. She is author of *Queer Notions* (Scarlet Press) and *Damn Fine Art by New Lesbian Artists* (Cassell). Her fiction was included in *The Anchor Book of New Irish Writing* in 2000. She wrote the screenplay for the short film *Salvage*, which was broadcast in Ireland. Her debut poetry collection *When the Lights Go Up* was published by Lagan Press in 2001. As Writer in Residence at HMP Bullwood Hall, she edited an anthology of women prisoners' writing called *A Strong Voice in a Small Space* (Cherry Picking Press), which won the Raymond Williams Community Publishing Award in 2003. Several poems appear in *Breaking the Skin* (Black Mountain Press) and the Apples and Snakes 21st Anniversary Anthology, *Velocity*. Her poetry also appears in *The North*, *Poetry Ireland Review* and *The Shop*. A pamphlet, *The Future of Something Delicate* was published by Smith/Doorstop in 2005 and a second collection is forthcoming in 2006. She teaches at the University of Greenwich.